the boy

book

(a study of habits and behaviors, plus techniques for taming them)

the boy book

e. lockhart

delacorte press

Published by Delacorte Press
an imprint of Random House Children's Books
a division of Random House, Inc.
New York

This is a work of fiction. Names, characters, places, and incidents either are the product
of the author's imagination or are used fictitiously. Any resemblance to
actual persons, living or dead, events, or locales is entirely coincidental.

Delacorte Press and colophon are registered trademarks of Random House, Inc.

Visit us on the Web! www.randomhouse.com/teens

Educators and librarians, for a variety of teaching tools, visit us at
www.randomhouse.com/teachers

The Library of Congress has cataloged the hardcover edition of this work as follows:

Lockhart, E.
The boy book: a study of habits and behaviors, plus techniques
for taming them / E. Lockhart.
p.   cm.
Companion to the author's The boyfriend list.
Summary: A high school junior continues her quest for relevant data
on the male species, while enjoying her freedom as a newly licensed driver and
examining her friendship with a clean-living vegetarian classmate.
ISBN: 978-0-385-73208-6 (trade)
ISBN: 978-0-385-90239-7 (GLB)
[1. Interpersonal relations–Fiction. 2. Dating (Social customs)–
Fiction. 3. Schools–Fiction. 4. High schools–Fiction.
5. Friendship–Fiction.] I. Title.
PZ7.L79757Boy 2006
[Fic]–dc22   2006004601

ISBN: 978-0-385-73209-3 (tr. pbk.)

Printed in the United States of America

10 9 8 7 6 5 4 3 2 1

First Trade Paperback Edition

For Zoe Jenkin

contents

1.

The Care and Ownership of Boobs

(a subject important to our study of the male humanoid animal because the boobs, if deployed properly, are like giant boy magnets attached to your chest.

Or smallish boy magnets. Or medium.

Depending on your endowment.

But boy magnets. *That* is the point.

They are magnets, we say. Magnets!)

1. If you jiggle, wear a bra. This means you. (Yes, you.) It is not anti-feminist. It is more comfy and keeps the boobs from getting floppy.
2. No matter how puny your frontal equipment, don't wear the kind with the giant pads inside. If a guy squeezes them, he will wonder why they feel like Nerf balls instead of boobs. And if you forget and wear a normal bra one day, everyone will then speculate on the

strange expanding and contracting nature of your boobage. (Reference: the mysteriously changing chestal profile of Madame Long, French teacher and sometime bra padder.)

3. A helpful hint: For optimal shape, go in the bathroom stall and hike them up inside the bra.

4. Do not perform the above maneuver in public, no matter how urgent you think it is.

5. Do not go topless in anyone's hot tub. Remember how Cricket had to press her chest against the side of the Van Deusens' tub for forty-five minutes when Gideon and his friends came home? Let that be a lesson to you. (Yes, you.)

6. Do not sunbathe topless either, unless you're completely ready to have sunburnt boobs whose skin will never be the same again (Reference: Roo, even though she swears she used sunblock) or unless you want to be yelled at by your mother for exposing yourself to the neighbors (Reference: Kim, even though really, no one saw and the neighbors were away on vacation).

—from *The Boy Book: A Study of Habits and Behaviors, Plus Techniques for Taming Them (A Kanga-Roo Production)*, written by me, Ruby Oliver, with number six added in Kim's handwriting. Approximate date: summer after freshman year.

the week before junior year began, the Doctors Yamamoto threw a ginormous going-away party for my ex-friend Kim.

I didn't go.

She is my ex-friend. Not my friend.

Kim Yamamoto was leaving to spend a semester at a

school in Tokyo, on an exchange program. She speaks fluent Japanese.

Her house has a big swimming pool, an even bigger yard, and a view of the Seattle skyline. On the eve of her going away, so I hear, her parents hired a sushi chef to come and chop up dead fish right in front of everyone, and the kids got hold of a few wine bottles. Supposedly, it was a great party.

I wouldn't know.

I do know that the following acts of ridiculousness were perpetrated that night, after the adults got tired and went to bed around eleven.

1. Someone chundered behind the garden shed and never confessed. There were a number of possible suspects.
2. People had handstand contests and it turns out Shiv Neel can walk on his hands.
3. With the party winding down and all the guys inside the house watching Letterman, Katarina Dolgen, Heidi Sussman and Ariel Olivieri wiggled out of their clothes and went skinny-dipping.
4. Nora Van Deusen decided to go in, too. She must have had some wine to do something like that. She's not usually a go-naked kind of girl.[1]
5. A group of guys came out onto the lawn and Nora's boobs were floating on top of the water as she sat on the steps of the pool. Everyone could see them.

---

[1] Nora was the only one of my old foursome (her, me, Cricket and Kim) who had never yet experienced some social or bodily horror related to taking her top off. See *The Boy Book* entry, above.

6. Shep Cabot, aka Cabbie, who squeezed my own relatively small boob last year with great expertise[2] but who is otherwise a lame human being as far as I can tell, snapped a photo—or at least pretended he did. Facts unclear upon initial reportage.

7. Nora grabbed her boobs and ran squealing into the house in search of a towel. Which was a bad idea, because she wasn't wearing anything except a pair of soggy blue panties. Cabbie snapped, or said he snapped, another photo. The rest of the girls stayed coyly in the pool until Nora, having got her wits together and wearing a pair of Kim's sweatpants and a T-shirt, came out and brought them towels.

I know all this because no one was talking about anything else on the first day of school.

Nobody spoke to me directly, of course. Because although I used to be reasonably popular, thanks to the horrific debacles of sophomore year—in which I lost not only my then-boyfriend, Jackson, but also my then-friends Cricket, Kim and Nora—I was a certifiable leper with a slutty reputation.

Meghan Flack, who carpools me to school, was my only friend.

Last year, Meghan and her hot senior boyfriend, Bick, spent every waking minute together, annoying all the girls who would have liked to date Bick, and also all the guys who didn't want to watch the two of them making out at the lunch table.

People hated Meghan. She was the girl you love to

---

[2] Yes, only one boob. Long story.

hate—not because she does anything mean or spiteful, but because she's naturally gorgeous, extremely oblivious, and completely boy-oriented. Because she licks her lips when she talks to guys, and pouts cutely, and all the guys stare at her like they can't pull their eyes away.

But I don't hate her now. She doesn't even bug me anymore. And she was lost on the first day of school junior year, because Bick had left for Harvard the week before.

So Meghan and I were standing in front of the mail cubbies when we heard a crew of newly minted senior girls discussing Kim's party and what happened. Then we heard more from the guys who sat behind us in American Literature, and then from a girl who is on the swim team with me. By the end of first period it was clear that Nora's boobs were going to be the major focus of nearly every conversation for the rest of the day.

Because Nora is stacked.

Really stacked.

She is just not a small girl.

She's on the basketball team, and she keeps those things in line by wearing a sports bra every day instead of a regular, so maybe you wouldn't notice unless you slept over at her house and saw them in the flesh. But once they pop out, they've popped. I don't like to use this language to describe the female body, but the right word for what Nora's got on her chest is *hooters*.

Nora Van Deusen is actually not the kind of girl guys tend to pay attention to. She's never had a boyfriend. She takes photographs and watches sports on TV. She laughs a lot and drinks her espresso black with no sugar. Her family goes to church.

And now, she was walking down the hall with her books clutched to her chest, looking down at the floor while guys called, "Don't hide that light under a bushel!" or, "Set 'em free, Van Deusen! Twins like that need a regular airing."

God, it was like they had never been forced to take American History & Politics, where we spent nearly half a semester on the history of feminism. Everyone should have known, after that, that it's completely retro and lame to make comments about other people's bodies in the hallway.

"Hey, Nora, can you fly me somewhere with those hot-air balloons?"

It was like they'd never seen a boob before.

And maybe they hadn't.

Besides the info Meghan and I got eavesdropping, the main person who filled me in was Noel DuBoise. He turned up in my Art History class and then again in Chemistry, where we decided to be lab partners as a way of lightening up what promised to be a painful semester of scientific suffering.

Here's Noel: blond, spiky hair that probably requires quantities of gel; nondrinker, clean liver, vegetarian but heavy smoker; pierced eyebrow; underweight; funny in a mutter-under-your-breath way. I'd known him forever, because everyone at Tate Prep has known each other since kindergarten,[3] but I really only made friends with him in Painting Elective last year, and then he stood by me during

---

[3] Tate Prep is where Seattle lawyers and Microsoft millionaires send their children. It has a small population and a big campus. I go on scholarship.

all the debacles of sophomore spring, when everyone acted like I was covered with the strange blue spots of leprosy.

Noel is one of those people who doesn't have a clique— but he isn't a leper, either. I used to wonder if he was gay, but he's completely not, though he definitely holds himself aloof from the rabidly hetero merry-go-round of our high school.

Noel looks at the Tate Universe as if he finds it all mildly amusing and sometimes a bit sickening, but he's willing to participate for purposes of research so that he can bring back interesting tidbits of information to the ironic, punk rock planet where he really lives.

People like him for this quality. They invite him to parties. He can sit at anyone's table. But he never really seems committed, if you know what I mean.

Noel and I hadn't seen each other all summer. I had been traveling with my mom during the first half.[4] Then, in August, he went to New York City to visit his older brother, Claude, who goes to Cooper Union.

Even when we were both in Seattle, Noel and I had never been the make-plans level of friends. More like Painting Elective friends who sometimes put notes in each other's mail cubbies.

We didn't call each other or anything.

At the end of the summer, though, Noel had sent me an e-mail. A New York City travel report.

7

---

[4] My mom is a performance artist. She spent last summer on a five-city tour of her new show, *Elaine Oliver: Twist and Shout!*

Number of stairs to Claude's walk-up apartment: seventy.

Number of lights in Times Square: a gazillion.

Number of dumplings consumed in a single sitting: eleven.

Number of times yours truly did not go to bed until four a.m.: eleven.

Number of times Claude called me a little punk: countless.

Number of gay dance clubs he dragged me to: three.

Name of person who busted out dancing and then fell on his little punk butt with all his brother's friends looking: Noel.

I wondered if he sent the e-mail to more than one person, but then I decided I didn't care. I had only one official friend (Meghan), and I couldn't afford to get huffy. So I wrote him back:

Number of Popsicles consumed in a single sitting: 3.5.

Number of times my dad said, "Where did those Popsicles go? I was sure I had some in here": six.

Person who is annoying me: my mother. Twenty seconds ago she went, "Ruby, I notice there is a lot of your stuff lying around the living room," because she read a book called *Empower Your Girl Child* that told her not to tell me to pick up my damn stuff, because that kind of authoritative directive subjugates me when I'm supposed to be developing my autonomy. Instead, she's supposed to remark on something I'm doing that she doesn't like, using the phrase "I notice," and then wait for me to make an independent decision to take the socially responsible action of . . . picking up my damn stuff.

Only I am wise to her wily parenting ways, because I read her book when she wasn't looking!

Person who is making me laugh right now: John Belushi.[5] (No, not here. That would be seriously weird and highly disturbing. On TV.)

Person I can see out my dad's office window: Hutch.[6]

Person who has her driver's license and permission to borrow the Honda on weekends:

Roo!

Roo!

Roo!

And Noel wrote back:

Why Hutch outside window?

And I wrote back:

He helps my dad in the greenhouse. Kevin Oliver = sole employee and proprietor of a gardening catalog/ newsletter/extremely boring publication entitled *Container Gardening for the Rare Bloom Lover.*

Hutch got a haircut.

---

[5] John Belushi was a comedian who used to be on *Saturday Night Live* (Cheese-buguh! Cheesebuguh!) and starred in *Animal House* and *The Blues Brothers*. He killed himself by accident doing too many drugs when he was only thirty-three. Like Elvis, but even grosser and also naked.

[6] Hutch: aka John Hutchinson. Goes to school with me. Given to quoting retro metal songs and not brushing his teeth. But he's all right.

Noel didn't reply. But on that first day of school he asked me to be his Chem lab partner. Even though we didn't have to do a lab until Thursday.

I nodded. After class, we headed toward the refectory for lunch, and Noel lit a cigarette, not caring if any teachers could see him.

I looked at his pale skin and his bony hand clutching the smoke, and he'd written "through page 40" on his knuckles in blue ink. I was thinking how good it was to see him, and how even though we hadn't seen each other all summer, maybe we'd be friends, at least of the hanging-out-at-school sort, and also how he was really quite cute in an anemic sort of way, when Noel tossed his cigarette in the garbage and grabbed my arm. We were ten yards from the refectory entrance.

"Just a sec," he said. "You can come with me if you want–" And he pulled me around the side of the building, behind a bush where no one could see us from the path.

I thought for a second he was going to kiss me
and I didn't know if I wanted him to
because I hadn't thought it was leading to that
even though we had held hands that one time at the Spring Fling afterparty
but maybe I did want it to lead to that–
and his pale neck looked beautiful
and his gray-green eyes had a sparkle
and yes, I did want to.

But would he really kiss me right there in the middle of the Tate campus, halfway to lunch?

And was it a good idea for a person (me) with a bad

reputation to be making out in the bushes on the first day of school?

Then Noel pulled an orange plastic tube out of his jacket pocket, inhaled, stuck it in his mouth and pressed the top down. He breathed in and out a few times, then put his hands on his knees and leaned forward, looking at the ground.

I could see the white skin of his back, between the top of his cords and his coat.

He stood up and puffed again.

He wasn't going to kiss me at all.

I felt like an idiot.

"Don't angst," Noel said, looking at my shocked face. "It's not crack."

"I know," I said, though I hadn't been sure. Not being a crack smoker myself.

"I probably should have explained ahead of time. It's kind of creepy to drag you into the bushes and force you to watch me inhale controlled substances." He stood up and shoved the tube back in his pocket.

"You're asthmatic," I said, after a second.

"Since I was four."[7]

"But you smoke."

"Yeah."

"That can't be good."

"No."

---

[7] *Asthmatic:* Here's what I found out later. Something like one in twenty kids in America have asthma. Basically, the muscles around the airways in your lungs tighten up and the airways get inflamed. Then you wheeze and cough and can't breathe. Attacks can be triggered by dust or pollen, or by viral infections or food allergies.

"Then why do it?"

Noel sighed. "Because it fucking annoys me. 'Noel, don't forget your medicine.' 'Noel, stay inside—it's dusty out today.' 'Noel, don't work yourself too hard.' 'Noel, check in with the nurse.' 'Noel, don't do this, don't do that.' "

"Harsh."

"It's like—I hate having restrictions. The doctor said I shouldn't go on overnights without a parent. I shouldn't go to summer camp. I shouldn't travel to dusty or polleny locations. She even said I shouldn't run cross-country. That I should pick something that doesn't push the lungs for such a long time."

"But you do run."

"Exactly. And I went to summer camp. And I travel without regard to the pollen count. Because I want to prove I can."

"The smoking is like that?"

"In a sick way, yeah." He laughed. "I don't want them telling me I can't."

"You're a madman."

"So they tell me." Noel changed the subject. "Hey, it's pizza day. You getting that, or salad bar?"

"What I want is one of those sticky buns," I answered.

We left the bushes and went into the refectory.

●

Had we just had some kind of moment? Not a kissing moment like I'd thought, but a little intimate thing where he was letting me in somehow?

Maybe Noel had told me a secret.

Or maybe he took all his friends—sophomore girls and

Painting Elective people, whoever (he was always hanging around with *someone*)—maybe he took all of them in the bushes too. In fact, maybe I was the last person in the Tate Universe to have the Noel DuBoise bush/puffer experience.

I couldn't tell.

We got on line. I ordered a sticky bun and made myself the same salad I always get: lettuce, raisins, fried Chinese noodles, baby corn, cheese, black olives, ranch dressing. Noel got pizza. I couldn't find Meghan, but I didn't know what her schedule was. Maybe she'd had lunch already.

We sat down at one of the junior tables.

Cricket and Nora were two rows over. My ex-friends. Where I would have been, if life had been different.

I felt a rush of gratitude to Noel for not leaving me to eat lunch alone on the first day of school.

He tossed his head in their direction. "I went to that Yamamoto thing last week," he said apologetically. "She invited me."

I shrugged. Kim had always thought Noel was cool.

"I know you wouldn't be caught dead there," he went on, giving me more credit than I deserved, "but I can give you a report if you want a little light entertainment."

Then he recapped the news about the skinny-dipping and the boobs, adding the details of the soggy blue panties and Cabbie's photographs.

"Oh my God!" I said, indignant on Nora's behalf. "He can't go showing those around school."

Noel leaned back in his chair. "I judge him capable of pretty much anything."

"Nora would be shattered."

"Yeah."

"I mean, more shattered than almost anyone else I know."

"So?" He shoved a piece of pizza crust into his mouth. "So what?"

"What are you gonna do about it?"

"Me?"

"Cabbie has got to be stopped."

"And you think I'm gonna stop him?"

"All right," said Noel. "What are *we* gonna do about it, then?"

By the time we stacked our trays by the kitchen door, Noel and I had formed the Hooter Rescue Commission, the purpose of which was to recover the photographs of Nora Van Deusen's private, personal boobs from the nefarious and nearly unstoppable Cabbie, aka Shep Cabot.

2.

Rules for Dating in a Small School

1. Don't kiss in the refectory or any other small, enclosed space. It annoys everyone.
2. Don't let your boyfriend walk with his hand on your butt, either. It is even more annoying than kissing.
3. If your friend has no date for Spring Fling and you already have one, you must do reconnaissance work and find out who might be available to take your friend.
4. Never, ever, kiss someone else's official boyfriend. If status is unclear, ask around and find out. Don't necessarily believe the boy on this question. Double-check your facts.
5. If your friend has already said she likes a boy, don't you go liking him too. She's got dibs.
6. That is—unless you're certain it is truly "meant to be." Because if

it's meant to be, it's meant to be, and who are we to stand in the way of true love, just because Tate is so stupidly small?

7. Don't ignore your friends if you've got a boyfriend. This school is too small for us not to notice your absence.

8. Tell your friends every little detail! We promise to keep it just between us.

—entry from *The Boy Book*, written by me, with Kim, Cricket and Nora leaning over my shoulder as I wrote. Approximate date: early October, sophomore year.

Kim Yamamoto had been my best friend since kindergarten. She is the only child of a brain surgeon and a cardiac surgeon, and has a warm way of talking to people that makes you feel like she really likes you.

And she did. Really like me.

Since I was Roo, she became Kanga. In the beginning, we played around doing the usual kid stuff together—dolls and soccer and jumping on the bed. Later, sleepovers and nail polish and boy bands and trying to do the splits. Kim has a real mouth on her when she's angry, and she yelled at anyone who made fun of my glasses. In middle school, she'd come to my house and stay for dinner whenever the Doctors Yamamoto were too tightly scheduled to pick her up.

Somewhere along the way, around fourth grade, we befriended curvy, bookish, laughing Nora, and then in eighth grade this girl called Cricket with white-blond hair and pastel clothes. None of us knew what to think of her when she first got to school, until she started making these fortune-tellers out of paper.

We had all given up paper fortune-tellers in sixth grade, but Cricket made them funny. "You will make out in the grass behind the refectory with the guy who sits nearest you in math." Or "You won't amount to much, but you'll see a lot of action."

So we decided we loved her, and the four of us went through Tate Prep in relative harmony and popularity–not ruling our class (Ariel, Katarina and Heidi did that), but not lepers, either.

One night late in eighth grade when I was sleeping over at Kim's, she and I started our joint notebook, which we kept until late sophomore year, when everything went wrong. In it, we wrote the most important bits of data we had on the male species. We decorated the notebook with silver wrapping paper, and deemed its all-important contents only for the eyes of the truly worthy. (That is, Cricket and Nora.)

We called it *The Boy Book: A Study of Habits and Behaviors, Plus Techniques for Taming Them* (*A Kanga-Roo Production*), like it was a nature book about wolverines or something.

Which it pretty much was.

The Boy Book was a work in progress. Most entries were never officially finished: we added on to a topic as new information came to light, or as new stuff happened to us. Cricket and Nora would read it and write comments in the margins. Sometimes we had to tape in extra sheets of paper to make room for a particularly important subject; other pages were scribbled over with pseudo jargon declaring an entry "disproven by scientific experiment" or saying that "studies now demonstrate contradictory findings! Ref. page 49."

The "Rules for Dating in a Small School" were written by me with help from everyone else during a brief but glorious period at the start of sophomore year when Cricket was going out (well, more like making out) with this guy Kaleb from her summer drama camp, Kim was going out with Finn the stud-muffin and I was going out with Jackson Clarke. Nora wasn't going out with anyone, but then, Nora didn't seem to want to, so that was okay. Anyhow, with this glut of boyfriends, we were feeling quite pleased with life.

We wrote the Rules partly because we were annoyed with Meghan, who had hooked up with Bick in the middle of the summer and was always necking with him or sitting in his lap in public places. But we also wrote them because we knew that having real and actual boyfriends might begin to split up our foursome if we didn't lay down some guidelines.

And we tried to stick to the rules.

But remember that one about how it's okay to steal someone's boyfriend if you think it's "meant to be"?

I thought up that stupid rule myself. And Kim followed it.

Here's what you need to know:

Jackson Clarke was my boyfriend for most of sophomore year. We were together. That was that.

Then Kim stole him. She felt that things with her and Jackson were "meant to be," and it was fate. She said she never touched him until he and I were broken up. She said she followed all the rules—and everyone (Cricket and Nora) thought I'd get over it.

But I didn't. I started having panic attacks—these horrible episodes where my heart was pounding and I couldn't breathe and I thought I was going to die, only I wasn't dying at all; I was just neurotic.[1] I had to start seeing a shrink.

When Kim went away on the weekend of a big dance, Jackson invited me to go to Spring Fling. As friends. For old times' sake. To make it up to me, because he felt so bad about what had happened.

We ended up alone in the moonlight, and I kissed him.

He kissed me back.

We got caught.

All my friends hated me for blatantly not following the Rules for Dating and for betraying Kim, and Kim—she hated me even more. I became a leper and a famous slut.

So I was starting junior year in a seriously compromised position. My status vis-à-vis the various people I used to hang out with was as follows:

1. Kim: Not speaking. But far away in Tokyo.
2. Cricket: Not speaking.
3. Katarina, Ariel and Heidi: Informally not speaking. Meaning they were probably talking crap behind my back, but would say hello if absolutely necessary.

---

[1] If anything like this happens to you, definitely see a doctor. It could be a symptom of something physically wrong, not necessarily a panic thing.

4. Nora: Speaking—sort of. She and I chatted a couple of times this summer when we bumped into each other outside of school. But she hadn't called me or anything.
5. Girls I knew from swim team and lacrosse (sporty girls): Speaking to say hello. But none of them had been my friends, really, anyway.
6. Noel: Didn't care what anyone thought.
7. Meghan: Didn't have any other friends.
8. Hutch: Didn't speak to anyone at school anyhow.
9. And Jackson. The big one: Not speaking.

That was the hardest part of going back to school this year. Seeing Jackson. Remembering how we'd noticed each other on the first day last year. Seeing his freckled arms reaching down to pick up his backpack and knowing I'd never touch them again. Seeing him sit there during assembly, talking to Kyle and Matt, as if he didn't even know I was in the room.

At one point on the second day of school, he was two people behind me on line for lunch, and I was so flustered I dropped my change purse and money fell all over the floor. I had to move my tray out of the way so other people could pay, and balance it under my arm while I bent down to try to get at least the quarters before I died of embarrassment.

No one offered to help.

Jackson didn't even turn around.

I left the pennies and nickels on the dirty tiles.

●

"It was like he didn't know I existed," I said to Doctor Z that afternoon. "Like my entire human body had ceased to be visible. Like the fact that he had ever even known me had been wiped from his mind."

"Did you *want* to talk to him?" she asked me.

"No, I didn't want to talk to him," I snapped. "Do you think he could have been turned into a pod-robot over the summer?"[2]

Doctor Z didn't answer. She rarely does when I say ridiculous stuff.

"Last night my mother said she thinks he never had any feelings to begin with and he's a horrible boy," I went on. "She saw him with his mom down at Pike Place Market and claimed she was disgusted at what an unexpressive individual he was and did I know if his mom had had a nose job or did her face always look that way."

"Um-hm."

"But then again, she never did like Mrs. Clarke, and she always gets into such a thing against anyone who's been mean to me," I said. "It's one of the hazards of being an only child. So I don't know that I credit her opinion." I picked at my fingernails while I talked. "Then my dad said, 'Elaine, he's a teenager,' and started going on about how conflicted and guilty Jackson must feel, and how he probably just seems like a pod-robot because he's got so many feelings inside that he doesn't know how to handle."

[2] Pod-robot. A person with no feelings or memory, but otherwise indistinguishable from a regular human. Possibly an alien life-form; possibly a robot. See *Invasion of the Body Snatchers. The Puppet Masters. Westworld.* The Terminator movies. *The Stepford Wives* (either version). *Solaris* (either version). *Village of the Damned.* (There are also lots of touchy-feely movies where the faux humans develop emotions, like *Bicentennial Man; I, Robot;* and *A.I.: Artificial Intelligence.* But those are *not* what Jackson reminded me of.)

"What did you say to that?" asked Doctor Z.

"Nothing. But my mom got mad that my dad was taking Jackson's side and my dad said he *wasn't* taking sides. That was the point, he was seeing *all* sides."

"And?"

"I pointed out that he couldn't say *all* sides, he had to say *both* sides, because there were only two."

Doctor Z cracked a smile. I love it when I get her to do that. She crossed her legs and let one Birkenstock sandal dangle off her sock foot. "I see," she said.

Doctor Z, by the way, is my shrink. The one I started seeing when I first had the panic attacks. I go to her twice a week.

She's African American and wears lots of crafty-type clothing on the order of batik blouses, bead necklaces and one superhorrible crocheted poncho. She wears glasses with red rims. Her office is next to a mall, in a medical building full of dermatologists and dentists, but she's decorated it so it's cozy.

I like her well enough, and there's no doubt I'm feeling better in the panic attack department, but she also annoys me no end. I used to angst about her writing down all kinds of shrinky-type things about me as soon as I left her office. Like:

"Ruby Oliver, focused on grammatical particulars when she should be thinking through the emotional resonances of her father's defense of ex-boyfriend,"

or "Ruby Oliver, leaving change on the refectory floor in symbolic expression of personal loss of said ex-boyfriend," or "Ruby Oliver, suffering from paranoid delusion that said ex-boyfriend is actually a pod-robot,"

or "Ruby Oliver, still obsessed with ex-boyfriend."

But now I've learned not to care. "I'm just glad I got through the first two days without having a panic thing," I said. "I had to do a little deep breathing now and then, but I didn't go mental."

"Um-hm."

"Don't you think I deserve a prize or maybe a small plaque? Perhaps a medal with my name engraved?"

"For what?"

"For getting through not only the first but the second day of school without a breakdown."

"Do you want me to congratulate you?"

"Yes," I said. "Why not?"

"Congratulations, Ruby," she said. "But I don't think you need my affirmation. Your own sense of well-being is what matters."

"When I dropped the money was the worst," I said. "I couldn't believe he didn't even turn around."

"What did you want him to do, Ruby?"

I had wanted him to see me as a damsel in distress and come to my aid and touch my hand and feel a rush of desire and remorse. I had wanted him to notice my legs in my fishnet stockings as I knelt on the floor to pick up the quarters. "Nothing," I said. "I just could feel him ignoring me from across the room. Only it was a different kind of ignoring from last year. Because Kim's gone, probably."

"Uh-huh."

"I'm doing Reginald[3] today," I said. "You can ignore me."

"I'm not going to ignore you," said Doctor Z, popping a square of Nicorette gum. "This is therapy. You have my complete attention."

My sixteenth birthday was in August. My parents took me out for dinner at a restaurant by the water that makes great fried zucchini and puts umbrellas in the drinks, and Meghan gave me a box with five lip gloss colors in it.

That was it.

But I did get my driver's license, and neither of my parents needed the car on Tuesday afternoon, so after the Doctor Z appointment I swung into the mall next door, jumped out to buy a blackberry smoothie from the frozen yogurt stand, got back in the Honda, and drove to an interview I had for a part-time job.

Not a lot of kids at Tate Prep have to work after school. They don't need the money. Finn Murphy, Kim's studmuffin ex-boyfriend, mans the counter at the B&O Espresso—this great coffee bar with amazing cakes and batik prints on all the tablecloths—but he's the only other person I know of on scholarship.

Me, I needed to work. And no way was I babysitting anymore. That kid was like a vomit machine.

The Woodland Park Zoo, where I had the interview, is extremely pretty. They keep the animals in these nice

---

[3] Reginald is the name I have for what Doctor Z would prefer I call "experiencing a grieving process" or "coping with the loss of my entire life, such as it was." Because phrases like *grieving process* make me gag.

naturalistic enclosures. And they have an internship program where you get paid a little honorarium and you muck out stalls or take school groups around, and learn about zookeeping.

I parked and found the administration building. A woman named Anya, who was wearing an ugly brown zoo uniform, took me into her office and sat me down on a hard folding chair. "Tell me about your work experience, Ruby."

"Babysitting is pretty much it," I said. "This would be my first real job."

"And what makes you want to join our team here at the zoo?"

Doctor Z had made a big pitch for my finding some alternative thing to spin my brain around on. I mean, I swim in fall and play lacrosse in spring, and I read mystery novels and watch way too many movies, but I didn't really have any *interests* that occupied my mental energies, as she put it, and with school starting I would now be forced to spend all day every day at the exact place where all the badness happened last year, a place that was still filled with psychological weirdness and horror—which then made me seriously in danger of spending all my free time fixating on stuff Jackson once said to me, or imagining him fooling around with Kim, or obsessing on what happened and what I could have done to make stuff turn out differently—or at least how I might have retained some smidgen of dignity. And when my mind goes round and round like that, I start to feel panicky.

So Doctor Z wanted me to have a distraction. At first she said I should consider a hobby, something creative, but when I said knitting and stuff like that makes me gag, she said she meant something that would occupy my thoughts.

"I'm interested in animals," I said to Anya. "In how they behave. I read this book, *The Hidden Life of Dogs*, about the social dynamics of all these dogs that live in this one house. One was the alpha dog, and he bossed the others around, but when he wasn't there the whole dynamic changed."

"Oh?"

"And I read how there were these gay penguins at a zoo in Berlin. A number of them, actually. And one of the penguin couples adopted a rock, instead of an egg, and they'd sit on it to keep it warm."

"Yes, I read about that," said Anya, and I wondered if she thought I was a complete idiot. I mean, I really was interested in this stuff, but a list of goofy factoids wasn't about to qualify me to muck out a goat pen or answer tour group questions on the food chain.

"Did you read about the polar bear that got depressed?" I babbled on. "I think it was in New York City. His name was Gus, and he was so miserable all alone in his cage that he started OCD-ing and he would swim back and forth for hours at a time, as if he couldn't stop."

She didn't say anything.

"They helped him out by giving him toys and putting his food in hard-to-reach places, so he had to like rip open this plastic jar to get the fish inside. And they gave him peanut butter, too—he'd lick it off whatever it was. So he had stuff to keep him entertained, and he stopped OCD-ing."

"Yes, we have toys for our polar bears here, as well," said Anya.

"But it makes me think," I said—because once I'm on a roll I don't stop; I'm like my mom that way—"It makes me think that zoos are problematic. I mean, I know they're important for education, and they get people to care about the animals in the first place so students will want to study them and so people can do stuff to prevent extinction. But if the animals are getting depressed, and they always seem to be having trouble mating in captivity, then there's got to be something horrible about zoos, as well. I mean, *I'd* be a madman if I was locked up somewhere with a bunch of polar bears staring at *me* all day."

Damn. Damn. Damn. Why did I have to say all that? Anya was going to think I was a complete antizoo loon, trying to get a job there so I could secretly unlock the cages and let the polar bears out to eat Seattle.

She looked down at the application I'd filled out and pursed her lips. "You're a junior at Tate Prep?" she asked.

"Yes," I answered, though there didn't seem to be much point anymore.

"That's a good school. Tell me about your studies."

I rambled on about my American History & Politics class from last year, and how I was actually cranked to take Am Lit now, and tried to sound semi-intelligent for ten minutes. Then we said goodbye.

When I got home, there was a message from Anya on the answering machine saying I had the internship, if I wanted it, and I could work every Saturday from noon until six, and Fridays after school.

She said she thought I had a real sympathy for animals, and that was what they were looking for.

To celebrate, my parents took me out for ice cream. My dad kept calling me Zookeeper Roo. Then I spent the evening reading over *The Hidden Life of Dogs*.

By the time I turned my light out, I hadn't thought about Jackson for nearly four hours.

3.

Your Business Is Our Business: A Pledge

We are your friends and *everything* is our business!

Just kidding.

Of course you have a right to privacy.

But in the pursuit of badly needed knowledge about the male of the species, we, the undersigned, do solemnly pledge to reveal in these pages any bit of relevant data on the subject at hand. That is, if you find out something about boys and you can benefit female-kind by explaining it, you will do so in this book.

Even if it is embarrassing.

For example, if you find out:

1. How to do the nether-regioning in a proper and sophisticated manner
2. Why some guys think it is cool to get drunk
3. Why they act different in front of their friends

4. What they say about us when we're not there
5. What they *do* when we're not there
6. Why they don't want to dance at a dance (Hello? It's a dance.)
7. Why they don't call when they say they will
8. Why they don't shave when they have wispy mustaches that are obviously ugly
9. Why they don't want to talk about feelings, or
10. Why they chew with their mouths open

   We need to know! And you must report back.
   We pledge to reveal all relevant information.
   Signed, in solidarity,
   Kanga, Roo, Cricket and Nora

—written by all of us. Approximate date: October of sophomore year.

the morning after I got the zoo job, an e-mail from Noel showed up in my inbox. Send time 12:34 a.m.:

THE VAN DEUSEN HOOTERS NEED YOUR HELP: A PLEDGE DRIVE
   No, they're not endangered. In fact, these rare but hardy hooters are flourishing in their native habitat and well supplied with the necessary support
   heh heh heh
   anyway
   The Van Deusen hooters are fortified with brassieres and whatever else they need for their daily maintenance.
   Their problem is the unlicensed reproduction and possible

circulation of their likeness and the likeness of their owner, wearing nothing but soggy blue cotton bikini panties.

Please donate to the cause. Everything will go directly to the retrieval of the unfortunate images. Suggested items that will be gratefully received by the commission:

telescopes
art supplies
combat boots
infrared goggles
and Fruit Roll-Ups.

I wrote back from my dad's computer while I ate a granola bar.

What about Hooter Rescue Squad, instead of Commission? Sounds more studly. How about a Saturday-morning cartoon: H.R.S!—we could rescue hooters in distress across the nation. There would be a beacon in the sky, like Batman has, only ours would be shaped like—well, you get my drift.

P.S. Do we have an actual plan? I have art supplies.

And Noel replied:

Plan is in the
um
planning stages.
Have stocked large quantities of Fruit Roll-Ups. Now we just need goggles.

"Roo, you parked too far from the curb." My mother looked out the window of our houseboat, making her judgment from a hundred yards away.

"I did not."

"You always do. It's your weakness as a driver."

Besides being a performance artist, my mom is a part-time copy editor, which she does from home. So she's around a lot. Unfortunately.

"Don't you think you should be more supportive of Roo's driving?" said my dad, pouring himself a bowl of cereal and glancing out the window. "Roo, you parked beautifully." He's been giving me meaningless compliments ever since *Empower Your Girl Child* told him he had to build up my self-esteem.

"You can't even see the Honda from here," I said.

"I can see enough to know you did just fine," said my dad.

Meghan pulled her Jeep up to the dock entrance. I escaped out the door.

"Coffee?" I slammed the Jeep door and shoved my backpack down behind the seat.

"Of course." She drove to the Starbucks drive-through window a couple of blocks away and ordered two vanilla cappuccinos to go.

"Bick sent me an e-mail yesterday," said Meghan as we pulled out and got onto the freeway. "He finally got his college account set up."

"What did he say?"

"I thought it would be better somehow," she said. "I mean, he calls me every day, and he says he misses me and all, but the e-mail was like, about parties and a list of what classes he's taking, which I already know."

"Maybe he's not a writing type," I offered. "Some guys aren't."

"I want something to hold on to, you know? Like I want to reread it when I miss him, only when I do, there's nothing that makes me feel any better." She made her voice lower to imitate Bick. "I didn't get to sleep till three and I have a wack headache. Gotta motor before the eating hall closes down breakfast."

"Blah blah blah," I said.

"He'll be home at Thanksgiving," said Meghan, "which is only two and a half months. Then Christmas and spring break. And next year, I can apply to Boston College or maybe Tufts, so we can be together."

"Why not apply to Harvard?"

"I'll never get in. I did too bad in German last year. Besides, I'm the kind of person who's all about relationships," said Meghan. "I mean, I'm going to college—of course I'm going to college—but it's more important to me to be with Bick. Our love is the key. Everything else will work around that, don't you think?" She paused to give the finger to the driver of a minivan that had just cut her off.

I was split between feeling envious of her having a real boyfriend—a boyfriend who called her every day and wanted to keep going out long-distance until she could join him in Cambridge—and a feeling of bitter pessimism regarding Meghan's whole situation that I probably should have been talking about in therapy.

I mean, if a person (me) was legitimately possessed of

mental health, wouldn't she be optimistic? She would trust what Bick said, and trust what Meghan said, and believe in the power of young love.

But I couldn't help thinking that:

1. Young love was foolish and all too often cruel.
2. Bick was extremely hot in a rugby-playing, scruffy-hair way—and there was a good possibility Harvard suffered a real dearth of genuinely studly guys. He was going to have a lot of temptation. Sexy Harvard librarian types were going to be throwing themselves at him right and left, whereas Meghan was stuck with the same old guys we've known since kindergarten.
3. Underneath her lip-licking, sexpot exterior, Meghan is no dummy. She gets As and Bs. She sings in the school choir. She runs track and she's a great golfer. Is it wrong that I wished she didn't think she was the kind of person who was "all about relationships"? She was acting like a complete throwback to the 1950s women we studied in American History & Politics last year: smart, accomplished women who gave up their aspirations in life to define themselves in terms of the men they married.
4. On the other hand, if she wanted to be all about relationships, why not let her, if that's what made her happy? Maybe I had no political point whatsoever, and I was just jealous.

"I bet you could get into Harvard," I said. "You should apply if you want to go."

"I don't know," Meghan said. "Bick says the girls there are supersmart."

"I can't think about college at this point," I groaned. "I'll be lucky to survive another day at Tate."

●

On Thursday, at the break after second period, there was a note in my mail cubby. My heart started pounding when I saw it.

Nora, maybe? She seemed less mad at me than Cricket.

Meghan? Probably not. We had just had Global Studies together.

Noel?

When I had it in my hand, I could see it was written on pale green paper that was very familiar. And it was folded in quarters, the way he always folded everything he wrote.

The note was from my ex. Jackson Clarke.

●

Last year, Jackson put notes in my cubby all the time. Funny stuff that he'd written while goofing off in class, or the night before as he was getting ready for bed.

Most days there had been something waiting in my cubby before lunch. And although we had arguments on the telephone, and there were so many, many little things near the end that made me feel insecure and oversensitive around him, the cubby notes were always easy. He liked to write, and could draw good cartoons. He had a favorite blue-black pen.

He knew how to make me laugh.

Then later, when I saw his quarter-folded green paper notes in Kim's mail cubby, the thought of them made me sick to my stomach. It was like he had taken something that was just between us and given it to my replacement.

One day, in the middle of all the horror that was going on sophomore year, I had found myself alone by the cubbies. I was late to class, so no one was in the halls.

In Kim's cubby was a note from Jackson.

I know it is completely wrong and also psycho, but I took it. I shoved it down in the pocket of my jeans, where it felt like it was burning a hole into my leg, and ran into a stall in the girls' bathroom to read it.

> K–
> *I'm in Global Studies, and I'm looking out the window*
> > *And I see you late for class because you went to buy*
> *a sticky bun.*
> > *You're licking the icing as you walk across the quad*
> > *And I like the way your tongue looks, licking,*
> > *And I like the way you walk,*
> > *as if you like the way your sandal-feet are tickled by*
> *the grass.*
> > *So it's like you're with me now,*
> > *as Kessler hands us out a pop quiz*
> > *and I haven't done the reading, 'cause*
> > *last night I was with you.*

Tears ran down my face and I had to stay in the bathroom for twenty minutes, blowing my nose, splashing water on my cheeks, putting on lip gloss, and then crying again and having to do it all over.

It seemed so wrong to see that note in Jackson's writing, that note with his blue-black pen, that note that only a month before would have been addressed to me, and to know it wasn't mine.

To know I'd never have another note like that, never again.

●

And now I had one. We hadn't spoken since the end of last March, and here, in my hand, was a note. I opened it.

> *Saw you from afar at Northgate yesterday.*
> *Proof: you were drinking a purple smoothie.*
> *Then you got in the Honda and drove away, you legal driver, you.*
> *Happy (late late late) birthday.*
> *Jackson*

At that moment—and I know this is certifiably insane—I missed Kim so much. It was Kim I'd always talked to about everything. She'd dissected Jackson's notes, analyzed his gifts, listened to the blow-by-blow of any argument we'd had.

If this was last year, Kim, Nora, and Cricket and I would have spent the entire lunch period discussing the possible meanings of Jackson's note, after which we'd have written a new entry in *The Boy Book*—if not several new entries.

I couldn't talk to Noel. He was a guy. Plus, he was on the cross-country team with Jackson, and they didn't like each other much, so he wouldn't be objective. And I couldn't talk to the girls from swimming. I didn't know them well enough. So I grabbed Meghan an hour later as we were going into Am Lit.

"Jackson wrote me a note," I whispered as the teacher[1] tinkered with the connection of his laptop to a projection screen. He was all cranked to show us these Web sites about Colonial Boston and Puritan women in preparation for reading *The Scarlet Letter*.[2] But he wasn't technically adept, so someone from the AV club was supposedly on his way over to help.

"What did it say?" whispered Meghan.

"Happy birthday."

"Is it your birthday?" Meghan smiled. "No, wait, I gave you something in August. Lip gloss."

"He saw me driving the car the other day, so he figured out I turned sixteen."

"That's so sweet!" Meghan has no eye for the subtleties and weirdnesses of human drama. "When I turned sixteen," she said, "Bick brought three dozen roses to my house at like six in the morning, and left them in a vase outside my bedroom door. He arranged it ahead of time with my mom."

I didn't say anything. Bick, Bick, Bick.

---

[1] Mr. James Wallace is actually my favorite teacher. He's from South Africa and has a tasty, clipped accent. He also coaches the swim team and has some serious shoulders. I wouldn't normally whisper in his class, but this was a verifiable emotional emergency.

[2] *The Scarlet Letter*. By Nathaniel Hawthorne. It's about this woman who commits adultery and gets forced to wear a scarlet letter *A* on her chest to proclaim her shame to everyone, all the time. No one will talk to her. She loses all her friends. And then the guy she slept with dumps her and acts like it never happened.

Do I need to tell you that I loved this book?

"He's like that," Meghan said, and turned her attention to the Bostonian Society Web site, which was finally up on Mr. Wallace's screen.

●

At lunch, I didn't see Jackson anywhere. Seniors drive off campus a lot and get lunch at Dick's Drive-In or wherever. Nora and Cricket were sitting with Katarina, who had started going out with the nefarious Cabbie shortly after he squeezed my boob in the movie theater, but had apparently dumped him over the summer.

I sat with Meghan, eating my ranch-dressing raisin salad, and listened to her talk about Bick.

Blah blah blah.

But when I saw Nora get up and grab her backpack, with Cricket and Katarina still sitting, I bussed my tray.

"Nora. Wait up." We were in the refectory foyer.

"Hey, Roo." She smiled. A good sign.

I felt like maybe I was supposed to make small talk. Ask her how the rest of her summer had been, discuss the classes I was taking. But I couldn't. "Can I show you something?"

"I guess. What?"

"Let's go outside."

It was gray out—Seattle is nearly always gray—but warm. We went out to the quad and sat on the grass. I pulled the note from my pocket.

Nora took it and read it in silence. Then she said, "Why are you showing me this?"

I wanted to be friends again.

I wanted to tell her about the Hooter Rescue Squad—for her to laugh and feel grateful.

I wanted her to say, in her Nora way, all the things she thought the note meant, all the things it didn't mean.

I wanted her to tell me if I should write back. And what I should say.

As if nothing bad had ever happened between her and me.

As if Kim was some random girl Jackson was dating, and not her friend.

I thought all that would be obvious. And I guess I thought she would do it. Just do it automatically, because I was Roo, and she was Nora.

"Kim is going to freak out when she hears," Nora muttered, not waiting for my answer.

"I didn't show it to you so you'd tell Kim," I said, taking the note back.

"Roo–"

"It's only a 'Happy birthday.' "

"Then why are you showing it to me?"

"I–"

"Because if Jackson's stepping out on Kim, or even thinking about it, I'm going to have to tell her. That's what friends do. We had a pledge."

"Why would you freak her out for nothing? He's not getting back with me."

"He's not?" Nora eyed me. "Roo, then I don't understand what this is about. Why are you putting me in the middle?"

"I'm not putting you in the middle." I felt like I might cry.

"Yes, you are," she said. "You're making me choose between lying to Kim and being nice to you. God, sometimes it's like you have no sense of how other people are going to react to what you do."

"I thought—" Anything I could say was going to make me sound like a pathetic leper.

"You thought what?"

"I thought we could talk about it," I said. "Like we used to talk about stuff. I needed someone who would understand."

"Look, Roo," said Nora, standing up. "I can't make you stop liking Jackson. It's a free country. You can like whoever you like."

"I don't like him."

"Whatever. It seems like you do."

"Well, I don't."

"What I'm saying is, you can do whatever you do and I can't stop you. But you can't go stealing other people's boyfriends and think people are going to like you for it. And you can't go putting me in the middle, because I'm just not going to be there."

I thought she was going to turn around and walk away, but she didn't. She stood still, looking at me like she thought I was going to say something.

Nora tries to be a good person. She believes in God. She does charity work. She would never want a guy she wasn't supposed to want.

"I can't tell if we're friends or not," I said finally. "You and me."

"I can't tell, either," she almost whispered.

"Are you going to tell Kim about the note?"

"I don't know." Nora picked at her fingernails. "I wish you hadn't put me in this position."

"Sorry."

"What *is* up with you guys?"

"Me and Jackson? I haven't talked to him. We haven't even said hi since June."

"For real?"

"For real."

"Well," she said. "Maybe you should just stay away from him."

"I probably should," I answered.

"I gotta get to class," said Nora, sighing.

"Yeah, me too."

And that was how we left it.

●

When I thought about it later, I realized that Nora *was* telling me who to like and what to do, even though she said she couldn't. "Like she was saying that if I stayed away from Jackson, we could maybe be friends again," I explained to Doctor Z at our Thursday-afternoon appointment.

"Um-hmm."

"Do you think she'll tell Kim?" I asked.

"I couldn't say."

"Do you think she'll tell Cricket? Because Cricket will tell Kim."

"Roo," said Doctor Z, leaning forward a bit. "We can't know or say what other people will do. *You* have to think what *you* want to do. What *you* can do to get the situation where you want it to be."

"I could tell Kim," I said. "I have her e-mail."

"Is that what you want?"

"I feel like it's what I'm *supposed* to do. Like that's the code we set up when we wrote *The Boy Book*. To tell each other everything. Even after what happened. Because if it was my boyfriend writing notes to other girls, I'd want my friends to tell me."

"You want to uphold the rules you laid out in *The Boy Book*."

"Yeah," I said. "Only if it was me, I also couldn't stand the suspense, thinking my faraway boyfriend might be stepping out. It would drive me certifiably insane, when probably there'd be no reason to even angst about it. I mean, Kim's in Tokyo. There's nothing she could even do."

"Are you saying maybe it isn't very nice to tell her?"

"I actually opened an e-mail to her today and started typing before I deleted it."

"It sounds like you want to tell her."

I was quiet for a minute. "I kind of want her to know."
Silence from Doctor Z.

"Because—I guess I want her to think he still likes me. It's like, Kim's got all the power. She's got Jackson, she's got Cricket, she's got Nora, she's got everything. And the only thing I've got that she doesn't have is this note."

"I see."

"So it's not out of the goodness of my heart that I'd tell her. It's actually out of the sour meanness of my soul."

"I don't think you have a sour, mean soul, Ruby."

"You don't?" I said. "Then I'm not sure you know me that well."

●

I didn't tell Kim. At least, not then. What I did do when I got home is e-mail Noel the following:

HOOTER RESCUE SQUAD UPDATE
    Mission abort! Mission abort!
    The hooters apparently want to take care of
themselves and do not need our help. Besides, it
has been several days, and if Cabbie hasn't brought
pictures to school, he's probably not going to.
    Yours sincerely, in solidarity and in defense of
hooters around the globe,
    Secret Hooter Agent Roo

He wrote back ten minutes later.

    What to do with surplus Fruit Roll-Ups and art
supplies?
    —SHAN (Secret Hooter Agent Noel)

That's what I like about guys (sometimes).

They don't ask you *why* Nora's hooters want to take
care of themselves. They don't read between the lines and
say, "What, did you and Nora have a fight?"

They ignore that stuff, or they don't see it at all, and
start trying to figure out your next mission.

4.

What to Wear When You Might Be Fooling Around

1. A shirt that buttons up the front, for obvious reasons.
2. A front-close bra. Also for obvious reasons.
3. Perfume, but not all over your neck. Right behind the ears and on the wrists only, because if you have it on your neck, your neck is going to taste yucky. Let us repeat: not on the neck.
4. Lip gloss—but never dark red lip*stick*. Or you'll both get covered with it.
5. No rings. (This from Cricket. She claims it has to do with adventuring to the nether regions but refuses to elaborate for those of us who don't know what she's talking about.)
6. No sneakers. They can be smelly even on the best of us, and if it gets to the point of shoes coming off, you don't want to have to get up and go put them in the other room.
7. And whatever you do, don't wear a dress. Because if you're not

nether-regioning each other, but you do want to give him upper-region access, the dress is going to pose a serious impediment. Yes, you could unzip the back of it and pull it down from the top. But that is dorky. So leave the dress in the closet.
P.S. Bring gum or breath mints. Not bubble gum.

—written by Kim and Roo, with nether-region addition from Cricket. Approximate date: February, sophomore year.

I wore a dress to school the next day. A vintage navy blue thing with roses embroidered around the bottom of the skirt. I also wore a pair of old Converse, two rings, a back-close bra, red lipstick and perfume on my neck. I chewed bubble gum.

I was untouchable.

I hadn't seen Jackson except from afar since he left the birthday note in my cubby. I had written him six notes and two e-mails back, but I ripped up the notes and deleted the e-mails without sending them. Because what could I say?

"Thanks for the birthday note"? Too formal.

"What, are you and Kim broken up now?" Obviously desperate and semihostile.

"I hate you I love you I hate you I love you"? True. But lame.

Finally, I had figured out what to write. (Yes, I knew I shouldn't write *anything*. I knew a mature girl would ignore his plea for forgiveness and attention. And an ethical girl wouldn't flirt with someone else's boyfriend.

But I couldn't quite do that.

He was Jackson Clarke. It was how I felt.)

So I wrote "Blackberry smoothies are the only kind worth drinking" and left it in his mail cubby.

But nothing was going to happen between us. We weren't even on speaking terms, and my outfit was all wrong on purpose.[1]

I looked for Jackson in the refectory later, but either we didn't have the same lunch on Fridays, or else he'd gone off campus. Nora said hi to me on the lunch line, and I said hi back, but I couldn't quite look her in the eye. I had a swim team meeting after school—the first of the year—and after that, I checked my mail cubby to see if Jackson had written.

There was a Fruit Roll-Up in there.

●

My internship at the Woodland Park Zoo started on Saturday, and Anya showed me around. In the Family Farm area, from nine o'clock to eleven, I was to stand

---

[1] "Sounds like you were dressing up," said Doctor Z, later.

"No," I said. "This was the anti-make-out outfit. Everything you're not supposed to wear if you want to hook up with a boy."

"Oh." Doctor Z was silent for a minute. "Lots of people would say that red lipstick and dresses and perfume are very attractive."

"It was an anti-Jackson outfit," I persisted. "So nothing could happen as a consequence of me writing him back."

"Do you think he knew that?"

"Um. No. It was more like insurance for myself," I said. "Like it proved I wasn't doing anything wrong."

"Uh-huh." Doctor Z crossed her legs.

"What?"

"I'm just listening to you, Ruby," said Doctor Z.

I didn't know what else to say. "I looked good, though," I finally admitted. "I don't usually wear lipstick."

around wearing a zoo polo shirt and answering questions. She gave me a handout with the names of all the animals and information on their feeding habits. I watched a fellow intern help kids get food from the dispensers.

The cow was named Maggie, the llamas were Laverne and Shirley, and the goats all had ridiculous names like Rasputin and Napoleon and Queen Anne. Anya said I'd do a training program the following Friday after school to learn more about Family Farm. At eleven I was supposed to report to a groundskeeper named Lewis and assist him with gardening stuff.

Lewis was a thin, blondish man with an unfortunate skinny mustache. He had me plant flowers near the zoo entrance. He got all cranked when I told him my dad was the proprietor and sole employee of *Container Gardening for the Rare Bloom Lover.*

I had a lunch break for an hour; then at two o'clock I reported back to Anya and she said that since I was a good speaker (!!) she was going to put me in a training session to be on the microphone at the Saturday-afternoon Humboldt penguin feeding. The training wouldn't be until the following week, so Anya walked me around the rest of the zoo. We ended up in the penguin room, which was dark and cool. Penguins were waddling around and hurtling themselves into the water. Anya showed me the closet where the microphone equipment was.

"You wheel it out on a cart and put it in this corner here," she said, pointing. "Then when the keepers come in with the fish, you read from a script we'll give you that tells some fun facts about the animals. I know you're interested in penguins," she said, giving me a look that said maybe

I was just interested in penguins' sexual orientation, "so I think this will be a rewarding part of the job for you."

"Oh sure," I said. "I'm all about penguins."

●

"You have a fan," I told my dad when I got home that evening. He and Hutch were messing around with a bunch of ugly bushes in the greenhouse on the southern side of our houseboat.

"I have many." Dad grinned.

"You do not."

"He does," put in Hutch. "People write him letters asking all kinds of questions."

"I am the Angus Young of container gardening," said my dad.[2]

"Oh, no," cried Hutch. "You're completely the Brian Johnson."[3]

"You think so?" asked Dad, flattered. "I don't know. That *Small Roses for Small Spaces* guy is giving me a run for my money."

"No comparison. He's all flash and no substance. He's the Sammy Hagar of container gardening, if he's anything at all."[4]

---

[2] Angus Young: lead guitarist of the band AC/DC, famous for wearing velvety shorts and a suit jacket onstage, like a British schoolboy. AC/DC is an ancient heavy metal band that my dad obsessed on in his youth. And still does, actually.

    Hutch encourages him. The two of them blast geriatric guitar-fiend bands while they plant obscure flowering herbage.

[3] Brian Johnson: AC/DC's lead singer.

[4] Sammy Hagar: another old rocker dude. Even less cool than the others, if that is possible. He fronted Van Halen for a while and was famous for a song called "I Can't Drive 55." (Can you believe I know this stuff? It's my dad's fault.)

"This guy at the zoo was all over me when he found out you were my dad," I said. "He does the plantings over there and I helped him put in some things by the front gate."

"Really?" My dad looked interested. "What are they planting?"

"I don't know. They weren't blooming yet."

"You don't *know* what you were planting? How could you not know what you were planting?"

I shrugged. "I planted what he gave me."

"Roo."

"What?"

"Nothing," he said. "Don't forget we're going to Juana's for dinner tonight."

●

Juana Martinez is my mom's best friend. She's a Cuban American playwright with four ex-husbands and thirteen dogs. Her son, Angelo, is a year ahead of me at school, but he goes to Garfield, which is public, so we live in different universes.

Angelo and I have a bit of a history together. But only a little bit. There was a moment last year, in the middle of the Spring Fling Debacle, when he gave me some flowers. I kissed him on the cheek to say thank you, and he kissed me on my cheek back, and this tingle ran down my spine— but it was in the middle of a party and all kinds of badness was going on with me and Jackson (and with nearly everyone else there too), so nothing ever came of it.

I hadn't seen him since that night. My family had been to Juana's for dinner, because we're always going to Juana's for dinner, but Angelo lives part-time with his father and he had been a junior counselor at a summer camp on one of the San Juan Islands for a couple months, plus I had traveled, so we hadn't had to face each other yet.

"Do I have to go?" I asked my mom, inside.

"Yes."

"Why? I have a ton of homework."

"It's the weekend, Roo. You can do your homework later. And I don't want you sitting home on Saturday night. It's bad for your psychology."

"Oh, like going out with my parents is any better?"

"It's a lot better," said my mom. "Juana is making corn pudding for you."

I love Juana's corn pudding.

"And she just finished a new play and she thinks maybe there's a part for me in it."

"That's supposed to make me want to go?"

She laughed. "Go for the corn pudding. Go to make your old mother happy."

●

Juana's kitchen was an absolute maelstrom when we got there. Corn on the floor, a big fish on the counter with its eyes googling up, dishes piled in the sink and chopped herbs in small piles on the counter. "I'm getting it under control!" she yelled, wiping her face with her hand and smearing grease across her cheek. "Kevin, chop the head off the salmon, will you?" She grabbed a butcher knife and held it out.

My dad looked aghast and started to back away.

"I'll do it," said my mother, taking the knife.

Juana kissed her on the cheek. "Slice it up the middle, too. It'll steam in ten minutes. I'm stuffing it with leeks.

The corn pudding's in the oven. I got bread from Paradise, the kind with black olives baked in. Oh, and there's cheese somewhere in the fridge. Kevin, if you're scared of the salmon, you can root around in there and find the Camembert. It needs to be unwrapped so it can breathe and get to room temperature before we eat it."

My parents went to work in the kitchen.

"Get yourself a pop, Roo," said Juana. "Angelo's down in the basement watching television."

I didn't want to see the head come off of the fish. I grabbed a Coke and headed downstairs.

Angelo was sitting on a fur-matted sofa with two Labradors and a Yorkie. He was watching some reality TV show. "Hey, hey," he said to me, half looking up.

He looked good—curly black hair, baggy clothes, brown skin with a bit of a tan leftover from summer camp. "Hey, hey, yourself," I said, sitting down next to him and snapping open my drink. I would have sat farther away, but dogs were taking up half the couch.

"This guy," said Angelo, pointing at the television, "he's got to crawl through a tunnel that's a foot and a half high—and filled with cockroaches."

"Sick."

"The girl who went before him chundered when she came out," he said. "It was brutal."

I looked at his profile. He has full lips and a strong nose. I thought of how the kids at summer camp must have looked up to him.

"I'm not too bad with bugs," I said. "But I draw the line at cockroaches."

He pressed his leg against mine. Just a bit, but I could feel the warmth of his thigh through his jeans.

I wondered if I should say something about all the weirdness back in April. Because I'd been talking to Doctor Z about how to make my "relationships" with other human beings better than they are—which is completely sucky—and I felt bad because of how I had treated Angelo that night when he gave me the flowers.

"You know that party," I mumbled. "On our dock? I really was glad you came. It was a horrible night, and I did a lot of things I regret."

"Yeah?"

"I can't even tell you. The repercussions were completely harsh. I know I was rude to you."

"De nada."

"What?"

"De nada. It's nothing."

"Oh. Sorry," I said. "I take French."

Angelo switched the channel to MTV. "No, it was all right. I started talking to this guy Shiv, you know him, yeah? We cut out after a while. Me and him and some other people drove back to his girlfriend's house and went in the hot tub."

"Ariel."

"Yeah, that was her. They had this big tub on a deck overlooking the city, and Ariel gave me her brother's suit to wear. So I had a posh night. Don't sweat it."

Almost everyone who goes to Tate Prep (except me) has a hot tub on their decks. Rich Seattle people are way into hot tubs. But Angelo doesn't live in the Tate Universe.

"Oh," I said. "Good."

And then I surprised myself.

I reached over and touched Angelo's chin. He turned to look at me, and I kissed him.

His skin was warmer than I expected, and he put his hand on my neck and kissed me back. I was wearing a shirt that buttoned up the front, and he right away undid a couple buttons and touched my left boob. I reached my hand in and opened the front-close bra so he could get the upper-region access.

It felt amazing. I hadn't kissed anybody since April, and I could tell from the start that Angelo knew what he was doing.

I didn't think about Jackson.

I didn't think about Nora.

I didn't think about my panic attacks, or my leprosy, or how weird it was that Angelo had hung out with Shiv Neel after my party.

I didn't think about anything. It was better than working at the zoo.

"Dinner!" Juana bellowed from the kitchen upstairs.

I sprang back and squashed a Labrador (I don't know its name) and it let out a surprised yelp. "Ag. Sorry," I said, leaning over to pet the dog's ear in apology.

My naked boob brushed against its fur. I had forgotten that my whole chest was hanging out. Angelo was looking at me, laughing.

Not what you want when a guy sees your boobs for the first time.

I sat up as quickly as I could and wrangled my frontal equipment back into my bra, then buttoned my shirt. "We better go up," I said.

"Coming!" he yelled to his mother. He stood and gestured at the stairs. "After you, my lady."

I ran my fingers through my hair and went up to dinner.

We had salmon with cilantro sauce (which I didn't eat because I'm a vegetarian), corn pudding and Camembert with olive bread. There was white wine, and Angelo and I were allowed to have some. Juana and my mom discussed theater. My boobs felt like they weren't properly arranged in my bra. One was squished off to the side and the other was halfway trapped under the underwire. My dad told everyone he was the Brian Johnson of container gardening and no one knew what he was talking about, after which he gave a long, involved history of AC/DC and the ins and outs of competition among members of the plant newsletter community.

Dogs wandered around our legs and Juana fed them salmon off her plate. There was a raspberry tart for dessert. Juana asked how my classes were at school.

Angelo didn't say much.

I didn't say much either.

●

What was all that about? I wondered, when I was finally alone in my (microscopic) bedroom.

Why had I kissed Angelo?

Did I like him? Did he like me?

Had that been a *thing* thing, or just a thing?

Was he going to call me?

Was I going to call him?

"Think about what you want from a situation," Doctor Z is always saying, "and then try to get it."

She says that to get me to stop being so passive.

Because I talk too much and think too much and don't take action to get what I want. Because I blurt stuff out that might be how I feel, but that isn't remotely conducive to decent human relations. Like with Jackson: "Why didn't you call me?" or "Why did you talk to Heidi so long at that party?"

Well, I had taken action, that's for sure. Even with Jackson, whom I had kissed all the time, I had never opened my own bra. I had always waited for him to do it. Like I thought he might not be in the mood for my boobs unless he went for them himself.

Which is idiotic, I know. Guys are always in the mood for boobs.

So I had taken action, and I got what I wanted, and I deserved many therapy bonus points, yeah?

Only: I hadn't even known I wanted it until it was already happening. And now that it had happened, I had no idea what I wanted next.

5.

Scamming: Our Brief and
Irregular History

For future citizens of the planet who may find this book on an archeological dig and have no idea what we're talking about, *scamming* is physical contact of a relatively advanced nature between two consenting teenagers who are not going out, and who probably never will go out, and who are just entertaining each other horizontally at a party or whatever.

Now the history:

1. Cricket and French camp guy. Time: summer before eighth grade. Location: la belle France. Level: upper-regioning, outside the clothes only.
2. Kim and Basil from middle school. Time: eighth grade. Location: outside at the Christmas dance. Level: lips.

3. Cricket and Sammy Levy. Time: eighth grade. Location: Sammy's dad's bedroom, Sammy's fourteenth birthday party. Level: tongue.

4. Nora and Ben Ambromowitz (details omitted as the whole thing was gross, claims Nora).

5. Nora and Gideon's friend what's-his-name from church camp who had the long hair. Time: summer after eighth grade. Location: Van Deusens' Fourth of July party, in the boat shed. Level: tongue.

6. Kim and Steve Buchannon. Time: ninth grade. Location: Spring Fling afterparty at Katarina's. Level: upper region.

7. Cricket and four different boys from drama camp, all of whom remain nameless at her request, to be referred to only as Hair Product Guy, Ear-Licking Guy, King Lear and Horse Face. Time: summer after ninth grade. Level: two tongue, two upper region.

—written in Kim's handwriting, by all of us. Approximate date: August before tenth grade, upon Cricket's return from drama camp.

note my absence from the *Brief and Irregular History*?

I never scammed with anyone.

Kim, Cricket and Nora had all kissed people by the end of seventh grade and made out at parties by the end of eighth grade.[1] But I didn't even kiss anyone—unless you count one completely unfortunate spin-the-bottle situation—

---

[1] If you look at the history, you'll see Nora didn't do anything in ninth grade. She got a lot of attention in eighth, partly due to having acquired those hooters before the rest of us had anything whatsoever up top. But she only scammed those two times and then pretty much gave up boys. I'm not really sure why. Ben Ambromowitz was gross, she says, but it's not like he traumatized her.

until November of freshman year. Shiv Neel and I had made out in an empty classroom—but that didn't count as scamming because we were technically going out at the time, short-lived though it was. After that and before Jackson, I did kiss this guy Billy at a toga party while we were waiting for the bathroom, but Cricket said that didn't count as scamming either, because the whole thing only lasted two seconds and we were standing up the whole time.

But now I had scammed!

However: I was reduced to having a single, solitary girlfriend to tell the story to. I was bursting at the seams with my scamming news all day Sunday—and Meghan wasn't answering her cell.

●

Monday morning, I found out why. She was all teary when I got into the Jeep.

"What's wrong?" I asked.

Meghan shook her head and bit her lip.

"You can tell me," I pressed—though truth be told, I wasn't a hundred percent sure I wanted to know. Meghan is loud about her personal life (like how she sees a shrink because her dad died and the shrink makes her tell details of her sex dreams) and at the same time clueless about relating to other people. She'll tell you when she has her period, and she'll tell you every single sentence Bick wrote in a note, even really private stuff, but she doesn't seem to see how *complicated* life is. She's surprisingly unaware of how much talking went on behind her back last year thanks to all her public make-out sessions with Bick, and she doesn't seem to know that licking her lips all the time when she's talking to guys is highly annoying to everyone except the guys themselves. The senior girls in Bick's set all hated her, and she was completely ignorant.

Meghan can't be counted on for any analysis of social awkwardness, the way Nora, Kim and Cricket could. And I could never talk to her about the Noel DuBoise bush/puffer experience. She'd just be all, "Ooh, poor Noel," and that's it.

"I'm okay." She sniffed.

"Is your mom bugging you about quitting golf?"

Meghan's mom is a serious golfer, and Meghan learned to play when she was five. But she bailed on the team this year. She's doing Yoga Elective instead.

"No. It's– Bick and I had a long conversation yesterday."

"What?"

"We didn't break up. I don't know why I'm so shattered."

"What happened?"

We pulled into Starbucks and ordered vanilla cappuccinos. "He gave me this speech about how things are in flux," said Meghan, handing over our cash at the window. "How relationships aren't a constant, how people have to grow and change with each other. He said we should redefine what we are together each day, depending on what makes us happy in that moment."

"And that means . . . what?"

"He's reading all this philosophy, he said. Like Carlos Castaneda."

"He's been in college two weeks. How much can he have read?"

"It wasn't for class. He started reading this before, in

the summer. It's all about being in the moment, and not being defined by social structures. Him and me, I mean. The boyfriend/girlfriend thing."

"So?"

"So we should just *be,* each day, as it makes us happy to be, right then."

I was quiet for a minute. "It sounds like he wants to squeeze it into some girl," I finally said.

Meghan's whole face contorted. The Jeep swerved as she started to cry, and a green VW nearly hit us when she veered into its lane. Tears were running down her face, and she was making these hacking, choking noises.

"Stop!" I cried. "We have to pull over."

Still sobbing, Meghan nodded and got off the freeway, then pulled into the parking lot of a 7-Eleven. I jumped out of the Jeep and went in to buy her chocolate while Meghan stayed behind the wheel. I got back in the car and put some peanut butter cups on the dashboard, but she just sat with her hands over her face, weeping.

"I'm sorry," I said. "I can't believe that came out of my mouth." I dug a crumpled tissue out of my backpack and handed it to her.

Meghan kept crying.

"Really. Erase the whole sordid thought from your mind. I'm obviously bitter breakup lady whose boyfriend dumped her months ago and she's still not over it."

She sobbed into the tissue.

"Meghan, please. I'm deluded by my own issues. I'm sure Bick doesn't want to squeeze it into anyone."

"But he does," cried Meghan, sniffling.

"He told you that?"

"Not exactly. But he said he wants to have the full college experience, and that I should feel free to see other guys. And that this is a more enlightened way to be going out because we can be more true to ourselves and that will make us more true to each other."

"He used the word *enlightened*?"

"Yeah."

"Was he smoking something?"

"Maybe. I don't know." She rested her head on the steering wheel.

"I don't see why the 'full college experience' has to include horizontal action," I muttered.

"He said he still wants to be my boyfriend. Because we're in love, and nothing we do will change that." Meghan wiped her eyes with the back of her hand, then looked at her watch. "We're going to be late for class."

"It's only Precal." We had a miniquiz that morning that I'd studied for, but I didn't say anything. "Don't angst."

"Okay. I just have choir."

"All right. So we can sit here."

"Yeah."

"I would be shattered if someone said that to me," I said after a minute. "Even if there's no one in particular he wants to squeeze."

"You would?"

"Absolutely."

"But I don't want to break up with him," she moaned. "I love him."

●

In Chemistry, Noel and I were mixing some something with some other something to create a reaction. The new something was supposed to turn pink when we put the first two somethings together. We had a periodic table of the elements.

It was unbelievably boring. You had to write up a three-page report in a special lab format to explain that you poured the contents of one beaker in with the contents of another.

"Thanks for the Roll-Up," I said after we'd finished the experiment.

"Think nothing of it," Noel answered, not even looking up from his report. "You know I have a remarkable surplus."

"Then we need to use it up. Do you have another mission for us?"

"I thought you were Mission Director."

"Me? Then what are you?"

"Master Hit Man."

"But you had a plan in the planning stages."

"Well." He looked serious. "I lied."

I laughed. "I don't know if we can limit ourselves to hooters. There may be other body parts that need our assistance. We shouldn't discriminate."

"Like what?" he said, still looking down at his paper so that Mr. Fleischman, the Chemistry teacher, wouldn't notice we weren't working. "Do you know some ankles that are in dire circumstances? Some victimized elbows?"

"No."

He raised his eyes briefly. "Roo, if you're not going to take the Rescue Squad seriously, we may have to impeach you."

"Is there a formal process?"

"I'm just saying. As Mission Director, you have a responsibility to research the needs of the community and plot the operations of the squad."

"Point taken," I answered. "Reconnaissance work will proceed immediately."

"Five more minutes," announced Mr. Fleischman. "Rinse your beakers in the sink and wipe down your counter. Finished labs are due in class on Wednesday."

●

When I got to my mail cubby at the end of the day, there was a piece of pale green paper, folded up into quarters.

It said: "Root beer floats are always better."

●

November Week at Tate Prep is an Upper School institution. Sometime in late September, you get a catalog that contains the same goofy introduction from the headmaster each year:

> Back in 1972, Tate Preparatory renewed its founding fathers' commitment to the environment and outdoor education. The school had become coeducational only two years earlier, and new headmaster Frank Patrickson decided that our school should "get with the times" and "break the lockstep."
>
> He arranged to suspend classes for two days in November, with everyone being encouraged to "do his or her own thing," connecting healthy bodies and healthy minds to the great outdoors. Students might build kites or hike Mount Rainier.
>
> These days, I am happy to report, our options have

expanded—and November Days has turned into Novem-
ber Week. Tate students go rafting on the Deschutes River,
learn to kayak on Barkley Sound, explore the lava caves
of Mount Saint Helens, or backpack in the Canyonlands.
They return to school refreshed, and with a reinvigorated
sense of the wonders of nature.

What the introduction doesn't say is that November Week activities are superexpensive. Next to each project description is a cost. Two hundred dollars for kayaking. Five hundred for rafting or Canyonlands.

Not a lot to the parents of my friends. But a lot to mine.

Each year when the catalog arrives, my mom gets mad, saying that Tate Prep charges so much money, we should have projects like these included in the tuition. Especially since you *have* to do November Week. It's not like you can skip.

"It's exploitative of my trust, that's all I'm saying," she argues, year after year.

"You don't even pay to send me there," I answer. "It's not exploiting *you* at all."

"Roo, it's the principle. You go to Tate, you should figure the school's programs are included in the price they quote you. It's enough I have to buy your lacrosse uniforms."

Then, each year, I ask if I can do the rafting expedition ($450), and she says no. Then I try for the lava caves ($350), and in the end I have to stay home and do the cheapest course in the catalog, which is Birds of the Great Northwest ($50).

What that means is every morning of November Week you get on a school bus with Ms. Harada, who teaches my Advanced Painting Elective this year, along with a few freshmen whose parents won't let them go away from home for a week.

You go to a state park. And you watch birds.

Freshman year, it was okay. Me and this girl Varsha Lakshman, who was new that year and swims butterfly, hung out a bit.

We all had rented binoculars and notebooks to record what birds we saw, and we hiked through various parks Harada took us to. We saw kinglets and nuthatches and pelicans down by the water. Varsha and I shared our lunches, and it seemed like we might be friends, but after November Week she settled in with the swim team girls and I went back to Cricket, Kim and Nora. Which was okay.[2]

But sophomore year, I was completely sullen through the whole thing. All my friends went river rafting, and Jackson and his friends went backpacking in the Canyonlands. Katarina, Heidi and Ariel did the lava caves. Varsha and the girls from swimming hiked Mount Rainier, and the girls from lacrosse did Be the Ball, which involved a lot of running and listening to motivational speakers.

---

[2] I play lacrosse in the spring, but for some reason none of the swim team girls do. They row crew instead. So I've never really bonded with them. They're very sporty, and I think they see me as some kind of thrift-store/fishnet girl who they can only really relate to when I'm in my bathing suit. They're nice enough at practice—even after the debacles of sophomore year. But I wouldn't call them my friends. Same with the lacrosse players.

And there I was, with a bunch of freshmen and one geeky junior guy whose name I never even knew, staring at the same old pelicans, going on the same old nature walks, with same old Harada enthusing on the beauties of nature and trying to get us to sketch landscapes with the colored-pencil set she carried around in her shoulder bag. Then I'd go home at night to hang out with my parents like a complete loser.

I didn't want to bird-watch. I wanted to kiss Jackson on the top of a mountain and sneak out of my tent at night to meet him in the dark and make out under the stars. Or raft down an icy river, laughing with my friends.

When everyone got home, they had pictures of themselves rappelling off the sides of cliffs, or sitting together on the edge of a rubber raft, or standing in front of Mount Saint Helens. Me, I had another notebook filled with sketches of pelicans and phonetically rendered spellings of birdcalls.

●

"Why are these courses so expensive?" my mother asked, yet again, when I showed her the catalog. "November Week should be included in tuition."

"Mom."

"I'm only saying, Roo."

"I'm making fifty dollars a week with the zoo job," I said. "What if I pay for it myself?"

"Roo, it'll take nine weeks for you to pay off one of these."

"I'm not bird-watching again."

"What about this one?" said my mom, pointing to a description in the catalog. "Plant a garden for Public School Eighty-one, a greening project."

"That's like what I do for Dad all the time. And I do it at the zoo. I don't want to plant."

"It's seventy-five dollars. Daddy and I will pay for that."

My father came in from the greenhouse. "Maybe we should consider it, Elaine," he said, washing his hands at the kitchen sink. "We send her to Tate to get an education. This nature experience is part of it. Plus, it's important for girls her age to bond with their peer group."

"It's too expensive." My mother shook her head. "Now that you've spent our entire savings on that greenhouse."

"Don't start. I've already laid out how it's going to pay for itself."

"Call it a cash-flow issue if you must, but these courses are way overpriced considering what we have in the account, plus she'll have to have rafting outfits and a backpack and whatnot."

"It's important for her to be with her friends."

"She doesn't even seem to *like* her friends anymore," said my mother. "Cricket and Nora haven't been over since school started."

Ag. I had sort of convinced myself my parents hadn't noticed my leprosy. "I'm sitting next to you, Mom, in case you hadn't noticed."

"That's exactly why she's got to go on one of these trips," argued my dad. "She's spending too much time alone. It'll be good for her self-esteem."

"Did you have a falling-out with them, honey?" my mother asked. "With Cricket, or Kim?"

"No," I lied. Since when were they actually observant?

"When I was sixteen," she said, leaning back in her

chair, "I had this girlfriend, Lisa. We were always falling out and making up again. It was practically like a relationship."

"Mom," I sighed. "I don't need to hear about your quasi-lesbianism right now."

"Ooh," squealed my mother. "Do you think it was kind of lesbian? It's normal for girls to have crushes on each other at that age."

"I wish I'd known you when you were sixteen." Dad came over and kissed her neck.

"You guys are going to make me chunder." I stood up from the kitchen table.

"Please, Roo." My mom pulled her hair into a ponytail, using a rubber band she yanked off her wrist. "It's normal to experiment with sexuality at your age. Ooh, Kevin!" She turned to my dad. "Maybe Roo's been questioning her orientation! Maybe that's why she's been having the panic things and doesn't have a boyfriend."

"Hello! I'm still here."

"Elaine, we shouldn't be prying into Roo's personal life. She's a teenager."

"Exactly. Thanks, Dad."

"If she wants to experiment," he went on, "we should support her without quizzing her about it."

More Ag.

"We'll still love you if you're a lesbian, Ruby," my dad continued.

"I wonder if Lisa turned out to be a lesbian," mused my mother. "Do you think it would turn up on Google?"

"This is not all about you, Elaine," scolded Dad. "Let's put the focus back on Roo."

"I don't *want* the focus," I said. "You can have it all, Mom, really."

"I am fine with it if you're a lesbian, Roo," announced my mom. "I have lots of gay friends."[3]

"Do you think the falling-out with Kim and those guys was because of that?" my dad wondered aloud. "Ruby, do you want to share with us any problems you're having with your friends?"

Ag! Ag! Ag!

I threw myself on the couch and pulled a pillow down on top of my head. "I just want to do something good for November Week!" I shouted. "I said I'd pay for it myself!"

Silence, for a moment.

My dad pulled out a chair and sat down. "You don't have to make such a fuss," he said finally. "All you have to do is ask."

●

Choosing a November Week activity, though, proved harder than I thought.

Meghan was doing Canyonlands, which didn't thrill me. It had only sounded good when I thought of going with Jackson. And besides, my parents would seriously object to buying me a hardcore backpack and the other paraphernalia I'd need.

No way was I doing whatever Katarina, Ariel and Heidi were doing. That would be a social nightmare. But I also had no way of finding out what their plans were so I could avoid them.

---

[3] This is true, actually. Gay men, especially, love my mother's performances, and lots of the people she knows from working in the theater are gay.

Part of me wanted to do whatever Jackson did, to see what would happen between us. But he was sure to be traveling in a posse with Kyle and Matt, and I could end up spending the whole time being ignored while he was manly-manly with the guys.

Anything involving a tent was out of the question. Unless I did Canyonlands with Meghan, I'd have no one to share with. And it didn't seem like Noel and I were at the point where we'd make our November Week plans together.

My best bet was Nora. But if Nora was with Cricket, as she probably would be, then she'd barely speak to me. Unless Cricket could be convinced to come around and be friends with me again.

Then again, I wasn't sure I wanted Cricket to come around anymore. We hadn't spoken in five months.

●

"What do *you* want to do?" asked Doctor Z at our session on Tuesday.

"That's what I'm saying. I don't *know*."

She was silent.

"You mean, what would I want to do if none of this social stuff existed?" I asked.

"Yes."

I thought. "The social stuff exists. I'm a leper. We lepers have to make carefully calculated decisions."

"You fought hard to go on one of these trips, Ruby," she said. "What are you hoping you'll get out of it?"

Part of me just wanted to be like the other kids at Tate. To not have money be such an obstacle. To just *go,* and not have to save and work and argue with my parents. To just have a group of friends, and all plan to go together, like it was nothing that had to be negotiated.

I kept my mouth shut.

"Let me put it another way," said Doctor Z. "What do you think of when you picture going on the Mount Saint Helens trip?"

"Being alone on the edge of a volcano, with no one to talk to."

"What about river rafting?"

"No one to sit with at lunch."

"Mount Rainier?"

"People talking crap about me."

"Who?"

"I don't know. Katarina. Whoever's there."

"Kayaking?"

"Sounds cold."

"All right. So that one's out. Be the Ball?"

"No way."

Doctor Z sighed. "What do you like to do? That's what I'm asking. What activity do you like to do?"

"I like to swim," I said. "And read. And watch movies. But can you imagine a catalog description for that? 'Exploring the Shallow Life: Students will enjoy a double feature of *Love Actually* and *Bridget Jones's Diary,* wallowing in the hotness of Hugh Grant and Colin Firth, followed by thrift-store shopping, intensive reading of mystery novels, and a dip in the pool. Evenings will be spent consuming Popsicles and experimenting with cosmetics.' "

Doctor Z smiled. "Very funny. But you didn't answer my question."

I sighed. "If there was a nonbird wildlife one, I'd want to do that. But overall, I'm not really a nature lady."

"Yet you're telling me you want to go."

"Yeah."

She went silent again, and I changed the subject. We talked about how annoying my mother was for the rest of the session.

●

In Am Lit on Wednesday, Mr. Wallace stopped our discussion ten minutes before the end of class to talk about November Week. "I'm doing something new this year," he announced. "Running my own show. As some of you know," he said, nodding at Cricket and Nora and a few others, "I assisted on the rafting expeditions the past two years. But this year, Mrs. Glass and I are doing a course called Canoe Island, and I hope you will all come join us."

I had seen Canoe Island listed in the catalog. All it said was "Expand your mind. Nourish your soul. $375."

I hadn't given it any thought.

Mr. Wallace went on to explain that the project involved going to a retreat on a tiny island in the San Juans, off the Seattle coast, where we'd read and discuss meaningful philosophical stuff in the mornings; then, in the afternoon, we'd swim in the pool, hike around the island and take turns making dinner. Evenings, we'd watch important movies from the history of cinema that would continue to spur our thought processes about the philosophical issues in the readings.

Movies. And swimming.

It was Exploring the Shallow Life, only deep.

So I told Wallace after class that I wanted to do it. Before I could chicken out.

He looked relieved and said I was the first person to sign up.

"Your catalog copy is too mysterious," I told him. "You have a PR problem."

Wallace laughed. "You can work on your flip turns while you're there if you want. It looks like Imari from the boys' team might come, so I'll coach in the afternoons."

That evening, I got my parents to write the check, and promised to pay them back three hundred dollars of it.

"I hope you have a real bonding experience with your peer group," said my father, squeezing me around the shoulders.

"I'm just relieved we don't have to buy her a backpack," said my mother.

Angelo Martinez called me that night, and our conversation went like this:

Him: Hey, Roo. It's Angelo.
Me: What's up?
Him: Not a lot. Just got in from playing basketball.
Me: Cool.
Him: Um. Listen.
Me: Yeah?
Him: I, ah, I wanted to say I had a good time the other day. The other night. It was nice.
Me: Oh, yeah. Sorry about squashing your dog.
Him: De nada. He can take it.

Me: At least it wasn't little Skipperdee.

Him: No. If you squashed her, she'd have bit you.

Me: Oh.

Him: I'm serious.

Me: Actually, I meant if I squashed her I might have killed her. She's so small.

Him: You don't know her like I do. She can take care of herself. Once I sat on this Yorkie we used to have called Stinky, and I broke her foot. I felt so bad.

Me: So. Hey.

Him: Hey.

Me: Nice of you to call.

Him: Yeah. Well. I didn't want to be, like, not calling after what happened.

Me: Oh, you didn't have to.

Him: But I did.

Me: Don't angst. You're quite the gentleman.

Him: Not if you ask my mom.

Me: I'm hardly your mom.

Him: No. (laughs under his breath) You are hardly my mom. (Silence. For too long.)

Me: Do you want to go for a drive?

Him: What, now?

Me: My parents are in all night. I can take the Honda for an hour or so, but I have to be back by ten.

Him: You mean go on a drive, and park?

Me: Exactly.

Him: I'm going out to the porch right now, with the portable.

Me: You're what?

Him: I'm on the porch now. Waiting.

And he clicked off.

I told my parents I was meeting Meghan at the B&O and drove to Angelo's. He got in the car.

We drove two blocks down to a parking lot next to a playground and made out for an hour, listening to stupid songs on the radio oldies station.

It was great.

Then I drove Angelo home. He kissed me goodbye.

"Don't say you'll call me," I said. "I don't want to have a calling/not-calling thing going on between us."

"Okay. I won't say it. But Roo?" He was halfway out the car door, silhouetted by a streetlamp.

"What?"

"You can call *me*."

6.

Levels of Boyfriends

1. Friend-Boy. The two of you are just friends.
2. Friend-Boy plus Unwanted Crush. You are just friends, but you can tell he likes you. It is highly annoying.
3. Friend-Boy plus Crush. You have a crush on him, but you're just friends. Sigh. (Note: *You* are probably being highly annoying.)
4. Hopeless Crush. You long for him from afar. He doesn't know you exist.
5. Friend-Boy plus Mutual Attraction. You are just friends, but maybe there is something more in the air.
6. Flirtation. But you are not friends.
7. Scamming Mate. You fool around, but you don't hang out. Ever.
8. Friends with Benefits. You fool around, and you do hang out, but you are not *going* out.

9. Boyfriend. You are going out!

10. Serious Boyfriend. You can see a future. The two of you are getting horizontal on a regular basis. You borrow his T-shirts.

—written in my handwriting, with some additions by Kim. Approximate date: September of sophomore year.

When I got home from being with Angelo, my parents were asleep in front of the television. I went straight to my room, dug out *The Boy Book* and read all our old entries. Because I had no one to talk to.

I remembered holing up with Kim, lying on our stomachs on her big double bed, writing and laughing. And the time we brought *The Boy Book* over to Cricket's house, and Nora made chocolate chip cookies, and I burned my hand taking them out of the oven, then had to dictate my contributions to the book because my fingers were too sore to hold a pen. And the time Cricket had the weird interaction with Billy Alexander and demanded that I bring the book to school so she could add an entry the next morning. And when Kim left it out on my parents' coffee table, and my dad was just picking it up to look at it when we came back in the room, and we grabbed it and ran away squealing.

I fell asleep with my face on the page dedicated to Levels of Boyfriends. I drooled a little and smudged the ink. At two a.m., I woke up, brushed my teeth and changed into pajamas, then went back to bed.

So Angelo. He was, at that moment, an SM. Scamming Mate. Possibly to be elevated to Friend with Benefits, possibly to be elevated to Boyfriend. Or possibly not.

It might be too strained, with our parents being friends. Or too weird, with our lives being so different. Hanging out with him had never been easy, the way it was with Jackson (my only real boyfriend, ever). Angelo and I usually watched TV for a bit and then ate dinner while tolerating boring grown-up conversation. I didn't even know that much about him, besides that he was a summer camp counselor, and liked reality TV, and was an expert in the boob-groping department.

I had been to his house a million times and had never seen his room.

So Noel. What was he?

Because I had to admit, we were flirting. Or at least, I felt something very close to disappointment when he didn't kiss me and used his asthma puffer instead.

Maybe he was FBMA, Friend-Boy plus Mutual Attraction. Or maybe FBC, Friend-Boy plus Crush. Me with a crush on him. Or maybe just a Friend-Boy.

It didn't feel like the crushes I'd had before, when I I had radar and could sense where the guy was from across a crowded room. Like when I had that crush on Nora's brother, Gideon, and I felt like I was always saying the wrong thing when I talked to him, and wondered what to wear every morning in case he suddenly noticed me.

But I did think about Noel a lot. I tried to think of ways to amuse him. And I appreciated the way he walked, like his limbs were put together loosely.

I *noticed* things in Noel that I didn't notice about guys who didn't interest me.

So Jackson. We didn't include ex-boyfriends on the list of levels. What can I say? We were naïve and unheart-broken back then.

I felt, if I had to give Jackson a type, like he was a Flirtation. Although we didn't speak, besides hello.

Sometimes I hated him. He had betrayed me and dumped me, and he wasn't the guy I'd thought he was back when we were going out. I felt like I was a better person than he was.

At those times, I decided that the notes he had written me since we broke up (just the two) were some attempt to rid his conscience of guilt. Like if Jackson could get me to be nice to him, then he could feel that what he'd done to me last year was really okay.

Other times, I felt like he and I had had this great relationship, and then someone (Kim) had interfered at a vulnerable moment when we had to decide whether to break up or say "love" or rip off all our clothes and do it.

If she hadn't interfered, Jackson and I would have stayed together and worked it out, and everything would have been wonderful.

Wouldn't it be good to have a happy ending now, after all that drama, with me and Jackson riding off into the sunset in his Dodge Dart Swinger?

Yes, it would.

The rest of the time, I thought, He has a girlfriend. He doesn't like me. So don't even think about it.

But I did think about it.

Jackson was there in my mind, all the time. Like a tumor.

●

In a surprise move, Cabbie brought his photos to school on Thursday. Nearly two weeks after Kim's party. I guess he hadn't finished the roll that night. Or he was drunk and forgot about the camera in his jacket pocket. Or something.

Anyway, he finally got them developed, and Darcy Andrews, this annoying guy I've never liked, had them when I got to Precal in the morning. He and a bunch of other boys were huddled over a desk, ogling.

I went to see what they were looking at, poking my head over someone's shoulder.

There was Nora, sitting on the steps of the pool, her enormous hooters highlighted by a flashbulb. She looked hot, except for her face, which was a picture of mortification. Her hands were over her chest but completely failed to cover anything, really. One nipple was sticking out, and the rest of the boobage looked sexily squashed.

The second picture was less flattering—she was running up the hill toward Kim's house, and the top of her head was cut off, but you could see her hooters from a side angle, her soggy panties drooping at the butt, and some mud on her legs as she stumbled across the grass.

There were other shots too, spread out on Darcy's desk. Guys with their arms around each other, laughing. Cricket and her gone-to-college boyfriend, Billy Alexander, lying on the grass. Katarina and Ariel, holding up pieces of sushi and waving. Kim, her hair cut shorter than the last time I'd seen her, giggling as Jackson kissed her neck.

Ag.

I did *not* need to see that. I wanted to run out of the class and be sick in the bathroom. My hands started shaking and the room was suddenly hot and stuffy.

But Nora was due in Precal any minute. And everyone could see her boobs.

Now was *not* the time to have a panic thing.

"Where did you get those?" I asked Darcy.

"They're from Yamamoto's party," he said. "Cabbie made double prints."

"He knew we'd all be grateful," laughed one of the guys.

"Van Deusen has a lot on deck," another said. "She should get out more."

"Ooh," I said, all innocent. "Can I see? Let me look!"

"I don't know," said Darcy.

"Please," I coaxed, scooting in next to him and leaning over flirtatiously. "Just for a sec. I love pictures."

He pulled them into a stack and handed them over. As soon as I got them, I yanked the Nora pictures from the bottom of the pile, dropped the others on the floor and ripped the ones of Nora into tiny pieces.

"Oliver!" barked Darcy. "What'd you go and do that for?"

"You have to ask?"

"Don't go all feminist on me," he muttered. "Geez."

"I wouldn't need to be feminist if you weren't such a pig."

"Why jump on me? Cabbie's the one who took them."

"You don't have to show them around," I answered. "That's so completely mean."

"She looks hot," he said. "What's the big deal? Lots of girls were going topless. If they didn't want us to look, they shouldn't have taken their shirts off."

"Not true," I said. "What if I showed pictures of your dick around school?"

One of the other guys laughed. "You have pictures of Darcy's dick? Darcy, Ruby, I never knew."

"Do you have lots of dick pictures, Ruby?" someone else asked.

"Maybe she does," muttered this guy Josh—a big luggy redheaded guy. (Recall my überslut reputation.)

"A whole collection, you moron," I spat back.

"She doesn't have mine," said Darcy, trying to laugh it off. "It's too big to fit in a photo."

"It takes a certain kind of girl to take dick pictures," Josh said. "Ruby, you want to photograph *this*?" He grabbed his crotch on the outside of his pants.

"Please. I couldn't find it if I tried."

"Oh, you'd find it, all right," said Josh. "I know you know where to look."

"How 'bout I send a team of explorers down there with infrared goggles and pickaxes, and give them a decade or two to hunt. See if they come up with anything," I said.

A murmur went up around me. "Harsh," I heard someone whisper.

I knew I had gone too far. Given what I'd said, there was no way anyone would ever forget what a famous slut I supposedly was. My life would never go back to normal now.

"God, Ruby," said Josh. "Why do you always have to be such a bitch to everyone?"

"Yeah," added Darcy. "Why do you have such a stick up your ass?"

"Leave her alone." It was Varsha Lakshman. She'd been sitting near the back with a couple of other girls from swim team, seemingly not even paying attention to the conversation. "She was standing up for her friend." Now she got up and walked over, tall and broad-shouldered.

"She's ripping up other people's private property, is what she's doing," said Darcy, collecting the pictures I'd dropped from the floor beneath his desk.

"You shouldn't have those pictures anyway," snapped Varsha.

Just then, the teacher bustled in, plunking her books down on the desk at the front of the room with a heavy plop. I mouthed "thank you" to Varsha as I went to my seat, but she didn't say anything back.

The guys all took their seats, and two seconds later, Nora ran in late and slid into a place near the back. A ripple of laughs went up as she did so.

"We're doing graphs today," the teacher announced, thumbing through her textbook. "Page forty-seven."

Darcy Andrews tossed me a note.

I didn't want to pick it up, but curiosity got the better of me.

Slut.

●

Nora laid low after class. She left as soon as Precal was over, and she wasn't in the refectory at lunch. I wondered if she cut for the day when she found out about the photos.

There's no Chemistry on Thursdays, so I didn't see Noel except from afar, but after sixth period there was a note in my cubby.

Hooter Rescue Squad, Official Memo
Dear SHAR,

It has come to our attention that despite your supposed abandonment of Mission Van Deusen, and also despite your neglect of your role as Mission Director, you have nevertheless acted heroically on behalf of the hooters.

In recognition of your efforts, we hereby grant you the official Rescue Squad medal of honor, which comes in the form of a large slice of pizza with the topping of your choice, to be consumed after swim practice today—or on the day of your choosing.

It's true, once you eat the pizza, you will have nothing to display on your mantelpiece, but hey—we are a low-rent organization. It's the best we can do.

Vehicular transport will await you outside the pool at 4:30 p.m. (Pacific time), unless you inform us otherwise.

Sincerely, and with my utmost congratulations,
SHAN

I had an appointment with Doctor Z after school. I was supposed to get a ride home with a girl from the team who lives kind of near me, then get the Honda and drive myself.

But Noel was waiting when I came out. He was sitting

on a lime green Vespa, holding an extra helmet. "I went home to pick it up," he said, handing the helmet to me.

I put it over my wet hair and got on the scooter. I wrapped my arms around Noel's waist. His coat was open, and I could feel the muscles of his abdomen through his T-shirt.

Noel swung the Vespa out of the school parking lot and onto the street.

I felt like there should be a sound track.

We went to Pagliacci's, this pizza place on the Ave in the U District. I got a slice with peppers and olives. Noel got plain. We put hot sprinkles and parmesan and oregano and garlic on our slices and took a booth.

"Darcy Andrews called me a slut this morning when I ripped up the picture," I told Noel.

"What did you call *him*?"

"A pig. Oh, and I might have said his dick was too small to locate even with infrared goggles."

Noel barked with laughter. "That part of the story is *not* circulating. Good for you."

"I wish I'd responded to the slut thing, though."

"What is there to say?"

"I don't know. Maybe 'I prefer *tart*'?"

"Tart is nice. It's a pastry."

"Maybe I could reclaim the word *slut*," I said. "Like gay people have reclaimed the word *queer*, so it's not a whatever."

"Epithet."

"Yeah. I could run around with signs. 'Slutty and Proud!' "

"Sluts of America Unite!"

"Exactly." I took a sip of my pop.

"Your mom could wear a T-shirt: 'I'm proud of my slutty kid.' " Noel fished around in his backpack for a pen. "Here, I'll design you a slut logo." He found a ballpoint and started to draw on a piece of notebook paper. A sketch of a woman wearing a superhero cape, glasses like mine and a strange pointy bra.

"I don't think I ever told you that none of the stuff people say about me is true," I blurted out.

"About the boyfriend list?"

"I was never with all those guys."

Noel shook his head. "I wouldn't care if you were."

"But I wasn't."

"Okay." He shoved some pizza in his mouth.

"Really, I wasn't."

He was being nice, but I couldn't tell if he believed me.

"There's stuff about Nora up in the boys' bathroom in Main," Noel said, when he finished chewing.

"Like what?"

"How hot she is, and how no one noticed before. Explicit statements pertaining to jugs. And messages to her, not that she'd ever read them."

"Such as?"

" 'Let the puppies out to play, Van Deusen!' 'Share the wealth.' 'More than a handful is the way to go.' "

"Oh God. Poor Nora."

"Cabbie's still got his first set of copies."

"I know. But I don't think she wants us to interfere."

"You didn't talk to her about ripping them up?"

"No."

"We should call her." He pulled his cell phone out of his coat pocket.[1] "Do you know the number?"

I did, but I didn't want to call it. What if she was mad at me for making a scene? "What am I gonna say? We've been e-mailing about your hooters?"

"No. Just have her come meet us for pizza."

The thought of doing that was scary.

"Come on," continued Noel. "She's gonna be completely freaked about today. She needs some cheesy goodness in her life."

"She's probably at Cricket's." Cricket's parents were never home.

"So if she is, she won't come. But maybe she's alone with her hooters." He laughed.

"I didn't even think you *liked* Nora that much," I said, stalling.

"I like anyone who doesn't play by the rules of the Tate Universe."

"And you don't think she does?"

He thought. "Maybe she used to. We all used to. But I see her alone a lot, is all."

I took the phone and punched in Nora's cell number. She answered on the second ring. "It's Roo," I said.

"Where are you?" she asked. "Whose phone are you using?"

"Noel's," I said, taking a deep breath. "We're at Pagliacci's. You want to come down?"

---

[1] Everyone at Tate Prep, even the fifth graders, has a cell phone. Everyone but me.

She was actually in the University Book Store, a couple of blocks away. Wasting time, looking at photography books. She came in and ordered a slice, then sat down with us.

We didn't talk about the hooters, or the pictures, or any of the Rescue Squad activities. There was no way we could get the photos back from Cabbie anyhow.

"What are you doing for November Week?" Nora asked Noel.

"I don't know. I did Be the Ball last year with some cross-country people. Coach pressured us into it. It was complete murder."

"I don't know, either," Nora said. "Cricket and Katarina and those guys are doing Mount Saint Helens, but so are Cabbie and Darcy. So I'm not that into it, after today."

"Enough said."

"I'm doing Canoe Island," I offered.

"Are you?" said Noel, sounding cranked. "With who?"

"No one. With myself."

"She loves Mr. Wallace with a mad passion," laughed Nora, sounding a bit like her old self.

"That's not it," I complained. "Well, maybe a little. But it sounds good, too."

"All right, then, I'm in." Noel put his hands on the table in a gesture of finality.

"You mean you're doing Canoe Island?"

"Yeah, sure. If you're going."

"I'll do it, too," said Nora, ripping the crust off her pizza. "If you guys are."

And that was it.

We were going to Canoe Island.

We were a "we."

For the first time in months, I didn't feel like a leper.

7.

Neanderthals on the Telephone:
Or, How to Converse

It has come to our attention here at *The Boy Book* that telephone conversations with members of the opposite sex are largely painful and awkward. Samples of this kind of crap can be found on page 14, "Traumatic Phone Calls, E-mails and Instant Messages," but the problem is so widespread that we have decided to write a new entry in hopes of not just complaining but actually remedying the situation.

We know what you are thinking. It is not girls who need lessons in how to talk on the telephone.

We are experts at it.

Some of us could even medal in it.

The problem is the boys. And they need to shape up.

True, true, true.

However.

The boys are not going to shape up. They are not going to read magazines or informational textbooks such as this one that tell them how to talk to girls on the telephone. And they are not going to magically figure out how to converse either. It is a demonstrated fact that even bona fide boyfriends such as Finn and Jackson and Kaleb are hit with paralyzing stupidity and boringness on the telephone, and *you*, my girlfriends, you are the only ones who can do anything about it.

Some tried-and-true tips:

1. No feelings. Not if you can possibly avoid it. Feelings in person only.
2. No long silences. The male of the species hates long silences. If he is silent, say, "I gotta go, I'll see you later." And hang up. This is mysterious and alluring. And if it is not, at least you don't have any more awkwardness.
3. Some people will tell you that you shouldn't call guys, you should wait for them to call you. Hello? This is the twenty-first century. We can call them.
4. But have a reason. Don't call "just to talk," because they have nothing to talk about. Have a story to tell them, or ask if they watched some TV show just now, or ask about homework, or make a plan for the weekend.

—written by me and Kim, in my handwriting. Approximate date: November of sophomore year, following a long and boring phone call with Jackson where I couldn't believe we were actually going out, we had so little to say to each other, and a conversation Kim had with Finn where she almost decided he was too much of a boring muffin to be her boyfriend anymore. There was a space at the bottom of the page where we'd hoped to add more tips—only we never thought of any.

When I called Angelo, I reread the instructions from *The Boy Book* before I did it.

I was supernervous, because I wanted to see him again. I mean, I wanted to make out with him again, frankly. Nothing beyond friendship seemed to be going on with Noel. And Jackson hadn't talked to me once.

I remembered the warm feeling of Angelo's lips on my neck, and the way he unbuttoned my shirt, and the perfect curve where his bottom lip connected to his chin. But I wasn't sure we had anything to say to each other.

I figured I'd ask him if he wanted to go see *Cry Baby,* this John Waters movie that was showing at the retro film place in the U District, and we could talk about John Waters maybe. Or Johnny Depp, or Iggy Pop, or Ricki Lake, who are all in it.

Juana answered the phone.

Ag. I had completely forgot that Juana would answer.

Now it was like I was broadcasting this thing with Angelo to our parents, which was a patently bad idea.

"Hi, Juana, it's Ruby. Is Angelo around?"

"Roo, no, he's at his dad's this week. You want the number there?"

"Oh, um, no that's okay. It's no big deal. I had a question to ask him."

"Ring him at Maximilian's," she said, giving me the number.

I wrote it down and hung up.

But I didn't call.

I sat there looking at the phone and thinking how if I called Angelo at his dad's, it would seem different. Not like just a thing that happened because our worlds collided, but a thing that I was *making* happen, a thing of more importance, a thing that was full of weight, instead of the light, airy, secrety thing we'd had so far.

While I was sitting there, the phone rang. "You get it!" yelled my mom from the bathroom, where she was drying off after a shower. My dad was sitting at his computer, printing out mailing labels for his catalog and writing pithy gardening tips for his newsletter. Lost in his world of miniature roses.

I picked it up. "Ruby, it's Doctor Z."

Oh my God.

I had blown off my appointment and never called.

"I'm calling to see if you want to reschedule the hour you missed."

"Oh, um." I was completely embarrassed. "I'm sorry, something came up."

"That's okay," she said. "But you do know I have to charge you for any sessions you miss without twelve hours' notice."

I hadn't known that.

My parents pay for the therapy, and Doctor Z doesn't charge them too much because she works on a sliding scale, meaning people pay what they can afford to pay. But I knew they would *not* be happy to be shelling out cash for Doctor Z to sit alone in her office while I ate pizza with Noel.

"I don't think I can," I answered. "I have to work at the zoo tomorrow afternoon and Saturday."

"Well then," she said, "I'll see you next Tuesday. I hope there wasn't any emergency?"

"No, nothing like that."

"Good. Tuesday it is, then," she said. "But Ruby?"

"Yes?"

"If you miss another appointment, I'm going to have to notify your parents."

●

Friday was all right. Better than before. Nora sat with me and Noel and Meghan at lunch. Meghan hadn't said any more about her new arrangement with Bick, and she didn't mention him quite as often as she used to before he started talking about enlightenment and the full college experience. I didn't feel like I could ask, "Hey, is your boyfriend squeezing it into anyone? Do you know for sure?"

So I didn't.

I spent Friday afternoon doing my penguin orientation at the zoo, learning to read from the script. "Humboldt penguins are endangered. They used to be hunted for meat, skins and the oil that comes from the layer of fat under the skin. Today, they are primarily threatened by commercial fishing." And "The sound penguins produce resembles the braying of donkeys. They also communicate with head and flipper waving."

Saturday I did the Family Farm orientation and helped Lewis put in some more plants. That night, I went to *Cry Baby* with Meghan, and we drove home swooning about how hot Johnny Depp was before he got old. Sunday, I wrote a paper and did a bunch of Precal homework and bothered my dad and Hutch in the greenhouse.

Around nine o'clock, the phone rang.

"My mom told me you called." It was Angelo.

"Oh, yeah, I did, a couple days ago."

"I was at my dad's."

"She told me."

"How was it?"

"Fine."

A long silence. The kind you're not supposed to have. But it wasn't my fault. He caught me unprepared.

"So what's up?" he finally said.

"Not much. I did homework all day."

"I mean, why'd you call?"

"I was gonna see if you wanted to see this movie, *Cry Baby.*"

"Maybe I do. What is it?"

"I already saw it," I said. "I went with my friend Meghan."

"Oh."

"Yeah."

"So."

"It was good."

"That's cool."

"It was like a fifties thing. A musical. But by John Waters, the guy who made *Pecker* and *Hairspray.*"

"Oh, yeah. That guy. I think I know who he is."

"With the skinny mustache."

"What? Maybe I don't know after all."

Another silence.

Was he hurt that I didn't call him at his dad's? Or that I went to the movie without him?

I didn't know how to bring it up, and even if I did, discussing feelings with a clear telephone Neanderthal like Angelo was out of the question.

And did I even want to be making out with a guy who didn't know who John Waters was?

"Okay, then," I said. "Well, thanks for calling me back. I gotta go."

"Sure. Bye."

We hung up.

A second later, the phone rang again. "Roo?" It was Angelo, calling back.

"Yeah?"

"Lemme give you my cell number. In case you want to call it. I mean, you don't have to, but if you do—"

"Sure," I said. "Let me get a pen."

I got one, and I wrote it down. "Okay, now I have it."

"Good," he said.

"Yeah, thanks."

"Later, then."

"Yeah."

Nothing from Angelo.

"I gotta go," I said.

"Okay. Bye."

Somehow, the tips from *The Boy Book* hadn't helped at all.

●

On Monday the gossip about Nora's hooters seemed to have died down, and Noel told me he covered all the stuff on the bathroom wall with a thick black marker. Tuesday, though, I was sitting on the front steps of the main building, trying to finish *The Scarlet Letter* for Am Lit, when Jackson plopped down next to me.

"Hey there, Ruby Oliver," he said.

"Hey there, Mr. Clarke."

Why was he sitting next to me? Why was he even talking to me?

Did I want him to talk to me?

"So what's new? I haven't seen you. How was your summer?"

"I went traveling with my mom. She was on tour with a show."

"Elaine." He said it in a knowing voice. "Did she drive you out of your tree?"

I loved how he used phrases like that. "Out of your tree." Phrases no one else ever used, like he got them from his grandpa. And I loved how he already knew all about my mom, and I didn't have to explain.

"A fair amount," I admitted. "But I got to see Big Sur and San Francisco and some other cool places."

He was acting like we were friends. Like everything was normal.

Maybe he thought that acting normal would *make* everything normal. Maybe he figured I didn't hold a grudge.

Maybe I shouldn't have been holding a grudge.

Shouldn't I have been *over* everything by then? If I was an individual possessed of decent mental health, wouldn't I just feel relaxed when my ex-boyfriend came by to say hello?

Or would a person of decent mental health be in touch with her anger and say, "Jackson, I don't think you're a good person and I don't want to pretend we're friends after what happened," and walk away?

If my mind had been functioning, I'd have either said *that* and never spoken to him again—or else I'd have had a calm, friendly conversation like no badness had ever happened.

But my mind doesn't function. I have no idea how anyone would do either one of those things.

And instead of being relaxed or angry, I was happy. So, so happy that Jackson wasn't being a pod-robot who didn't even know I existed, because when he did that (as he had been doing ever since the school year started and even since he'd written me the notes), I felt completely erased. Like I had been this girl Ruby with pretty legs and a boyfriend, and now I was nothing—a space where a human being once was.

It had been even worse since the notes, actually, because it was like there was some tiny bit of Jackson that saw me and remembered, but most of him was a pod-robot. Because of the notes, I could never get used to it, the way I might have if he was consistent, and whenever the pod-robot passed me in the hallway and didn't even glance at me, the erased feeling would flood over me again like it was new.

"I've been to San Francisco," he said. "I'm thinking about applying to Berkeley."

"That's cool," I said. "It's supposed to be great." I looked down at my legs. I was wearing fishnets, and felt perversely glad. I crossed one knee over the other and saw Jackson's eyes glance down.

Kim Yamamoto has traveled all over the world and can sail and knows all about different kinds of food. She is richer and more glamorous than me, plus she has a flat stomach and no glasses.

Compared to her, I don't have much to offer, besides

nicer legs. But maybe I could be the wacky, unpredictable girl; the kind who always fascinates more conservative men in the movies.[1] Maybe I could derail him from his straight-arrow path and make him fall madly in love with my quirky free spirit.

"Are you going to Kyle's party Saturday?" Jackson asked.

This was the first I'd heard of it. And if I went to the party, it was sure to be a nightmare. But that is not what quirky free-spirit girl would be thinking about. "Maybe," I lied. "I might have plans with my boyfriend."

Jackson looked surprised. "You have a boyfriend? That's great, Roo. That's excellent."

"He goes to Garfield," I said. "His name is Angelo. I think maybe you saw him at the Spring Fling afterparty?"

"Oh," said Jackson. "Yeah, maybe I did."

"We've been seeing a good amount of each other," I went on. Hating myself as I said it, but loving the look on Jackson's face.

"Well," said Jackson, getting to his feet. "Angelo's a lucky man."

●

"I don't know why I lied," I told Doctor Z on that afternoon.

---

[1]Movies where a wild girl enchants and disrupts the life of an otherwise ordinary (but still attractive) man: *Along Came Polly. Something Wild. Pretty Woman. Addicted to Love. Bringing Up Baby. Chasing Amy. What's Up, Doc?. Cabaret. The Seven Year Itch. Garden State. Eternal Sunshine of the Spotless Mind. Moulin Rouge. Breakfast at Tiffany's. My Fair Lady. Funny Face. Annie Hall. Sleeper* (okay, so Woody Allen is not attractive or ordinary, but still).

She smiled in a condescending way. "You don't?"

"Okay, I do."

"Why did you?"

"I wanted to hurt his feelings."

"And?"

"Because it almost seems like Jackson *wanted* me to be heartbroken and lovelorn, and now he thinks I'm not. So now he's disappointed that I'm not carrying a torch for him."

"Uh-huh."

"He's always known in the back of his mind that he could be with me again if he wanted, and the part of him that's not a pod-robot would like to keep that as an option. Going out with me, I mean. Like some part of him is holding on to this connection we used to have."

"Because he wrote you those notes?"

"Yeah. Which shows he still likes me. But on the other hand, it seems like he wants me to be perfectly okay and happy without him, because that would mean he didn't do anything wrong. So maybe by pretending I had a boyfriend, I was really telling him exactly what he wanted to hear." I sighed. "I don't know."

"Are you saying you lied to make him more interested? Or you lied to put him at ease?"

"God," I snapped. "It was one tiny lie. Not a huge deal."

"Okay," she said. "I'm just trying to get at what's behind it."

"Like I told you, I lied to hurt his feelings."

"Um-hum."

"So, that's what it is."

Doctor Z put a piece of Nicorette gum in her mouth. "Ruby, we should talk over why you missed your session last Thursday."

Doctor Z never changes the subject. She usually lets me drive the course of the conversation.

I shrugged. "I just didn't feel like I needed to come."

"You didn't feel like you needed to come."

"My friend Noel invited me for pizza. And I have practically no friends, so I really wanted to."

"Um-hum."

"Are you mad at me?"

"No."

"Because it seems like you're mad at me."

"No."

"And my parents will pay you for the session."

"It's not about that. It's about your commitment to the therapeutic process."

I took a deep breath. "Do you think I still need to be coming here?"

Doctor Z sighed. "I think you still have some issues to discuss, yes, but fundamentally, it's up to you. And your parents."

"It takes up a lot of time."

"Yes, it does."

"I feel like you're saying I'm making bad choices. Like I shouldn't be going for pizza with Noel, and I shouldn't have lied to Jackson, or flirted with him, or sent him notes, and I shouldn't be fooling around with Angelo. Like you think I'm ruining my life."

"I didn't say that, Ruby."

"I know," I said, fiddling with the hem of my skirt. "But that's what it seems like you think."

Doctor Z leaned forward in her chair and put on an earnest face. "I'm not here to judge you."

"Yeah, but you're making me feel bad."

"Ruby," she said. "You are the only one who can make yourself feel bad."

"That's not true."

She was silent. We looked at each other for a while. Then I looked at the second hand of the clock going around in circles. "I don't think we've talked about Angelo in a long time," she finally offered.

"That's because I don't think you'll approve!" I cried. "You'll think I'm being slutty, or making bad choices, or using him, or getting used."

"I'm not here to approve or disapprove," Doctor Z said calmly.

"Right." I was being sarcastic.

"I'm not. I'm here to help you figure out what you feel."

"Well, I feel like you won't approve of what's going on with Angelo, and that's why I'm not telling you about it." I crossed my arms.

"Do you know what transference is, Ruby?" asked Doctor Z.

"No."

"Transference is when a therapy patient begins to relate to the therapist as if she were someone else in the patient's life. Feelings toward someone *else* are redirected at the therapist."

"Ugh."

"It's a normal part of this process."

"I hate it when you get all therapy-speaky on me."

"Okay. I'm saying that it's possible you might be angry at yourself, or angry at someone else in your life."

"You just don't want me to be angry at *you*, so you're bringing up this transference thing. But it *is* you who's pissing me off," I said, "and it *is* you who's making me feel bad."

"It's fine for you to be angry at me, if that's what you genuinely are."

"The hell it is," I said.

We sat there for another five minutes, in silence. Then the hour was up.

"I don't want to come back on Thursday," I said as I stood up to leave. "I don't think I want to come back at all."

I drove home crying. Everything seemed so messed up. When I got to my room, I tried to organize my thoughts.

How I Feel: a list of possibilities
1. *Proud of self for leaving therapy when it is a big waste of my time.*
2. *Pissed at self for leaving therapy when I am clearly a basket case in desperate need of professional help.*
3. *Proud of self for telling Doctor Z how I felt about her bad attitude.*
4. *Pissed at self for not even knowing what I'm really mad about.*

5. *Proud of self for going after Jackson, trying to get what I want.*
6. *Pissed at self for lying to him and being manipulative.*
7. *Pissed at self for trying to get another girl's boyfriend.*
8. *Proud of self for being forward with Angelo (sometimes) and having excellent scamming adventures.*
9. *Pissed at self for using Angelo (but am I using him? Don't know).*
10. *Pissed at self for indecisiveness and possible sluttiness in regard to liking two (if not three) boys (since am being honest, can't deny feelings of attraction to Noel) at the same time.*
11. *Proud of self for making friends with Noel and making up with Nora.*
12. *Proud of self for choosing Canoe Island without regard to who else is doing it and whether they will eat lunch with me, which translates into*
13. *Proud of self for progress in therapy (no more panic attacks, and other personal growth–type things), which then downward spirals into*
14. *Pissed at self for ruining therapy, which is the only way I have stayed out of the asylum these past six months.*

Then my mom banged on the door to tell me dinner was ready, and I told my parents I quit therapy, and they actually managed to keep their mouths shut while we ate, but later I could hear them arguing about it, after I went to bed.

My dad was saying maybe I'd come through a difficult time and was ready to move forward into self-sufficiency, which is, after all, the essential process of adolescence.

And my mother was saying, "Kevin. Be real. Ruby is neurotic and I don't want her having those panic things again, plus she's obviously got some sexual issues. I want her in therapy."

Guess who won?

●

The next day after school, Mom told me she'd made an appointment for me the following week to see a psycho-therapist in our zip code who takes our health insurance. "I want you to try it," she said. "If you don't like Doctor Z anymore, fine. But I want you to see how it is with this guy. Besides, he's only eight blocks away, so you wouldn't have to take the Honda, which I don't mind telling you will make my life easier."

"Mom, the point was that I quit."

She waved her hands in exasperation. "Don't be a quitter."

"I'm not a quitter. I'm quitting *this*."

"This is not a conversation we are having, Ruby. You have to go to therapy."

"I haven't had a panic thing in ages."

"You have to work out your issues," said my mother. "End of discussion."

I left the house and slammed the door and went over to Meghan's, where she told me how her shrink told her that her dream of being naked in front of everyone in her Precal class was a wish-fulfillment fantasy, which made Doctor Z seem pretty good by comparison.

●

When I got home late at night, there was a message on our machine from Jackson. "You should come to Kyle's party," he said. "Just in case you don't have the address, I'm leaving it for you."

But of course he knew I had the address already. It was in the school directory.

8

Boy-Speak: Introduction to a Foreign Language

What he says: I never felt this way before.
What is understood: He loves me!
What he means: Can we get to the nether regions now?

What he says: I'll call you.
What is understood: He'll call me.
What he means: I don't want to see you again.

What he says: It's not you, it's me.
What is understood: He's got some meaningful problem going on in his
    life that's blocking him from being anyone's boyfriend, even mine,
    though he likes me so much.
What he means: I like someone else.

What he says: We're just really good friends.

What is understood: Nothing is going on between him and that other girl.

What he means: We have a flirtation, but I don't want you to bug me.

What he says: I'm so messed up.

What is understood: He needs my support and help.

What he means: I want you to leave me alone.

—written by me, Cricket and Nora the Monday after Jackson broke up with me. Approximate date: April of sophomore year.

i was seriously thinking about going to Kyle's party.

Of course, I knew there would be all kinds of horrific situations there, but hey—they wouldn't be much worse than what I encountered at school on any given day.

1. Guys who think I'm a slut and make catcalls at me.
2. Guys who think I'm a feminist hysteric and a bitch because I ripped up Cabbie's pictures.
3. Girls who think I'm a slut trying to steal their boyfriends.
4. Girls who think I'm a leper and that the strange blue spots of leprosy will infect them if they so much as give me the time of day.

But I figured I'd go with Nora, if she was up for it, and maybe she'd ease the way for me. Meghan wanted to go, because she was trying to keep herself distracted from the

Bick situation. And some swim team girls would be there, and they were always reasonably nice.

And Jackson.

He wanted me to be there. And that made me want to be there too.

But that all changed on Saturday afternoon.

●

I was at my zoo job. I'd spent the morning at the Family Farm, helping toddlers get food out of the dispensers and answering questions about the names of the llamas and the breeds of the goats. It was actually fun. I pet the soft gray necks of the llamas and fed Maggie the cow a handful of pellet treats. Her tongue was slimy when she licked them off my fingers.

Then I helped Lewis in the greenhouse for a bit, watering stuff and pruning a little, and ate my brown-bag lunch by the elephant enclosure, watching a baby elephant trail around after its mother.

Two o'clock was the penguin feeding. I had my script memorized, but I also had a printout of it folded up in my pocket. Anya met me by the door of the AV closet and got me set up, since it was my first time being official penguin announcer. The feeding schedule was posted all around the zoo, so a few minutes before we were supposed to start, visitors began crowding in around the penguins, watching them swimming their fat bodies through the blue water.

The room was dark, and penguins on the land part of the enclosure seemed to sense that feeding time was near: a good number of them had waddled over to the door, waiting for the keepers to come out with buckets of fish.

I stood on a footstool and started my talk when Anya

gave me the sign to go ahead. "Welcome to the Woodland Park Zoo's Humboldt penguin feeding. You'll notice that Humboldts are medium-sized penguins, averaging twenty-eight inches long and weighing about nine pounds. You can distinguish them from other penguins by the black band of feathers across their chests and by the splotchy pink patches on their faces and feet. The pink parts are bare skin, which is an adaptation that keeps these warm-weather penguins nice and cool. Humboldts are native to the coastal regions of Peru and Chile."

I looked up from my paper as the keepers entered the enclosure wearing knee-high rubber boots. Penguins started hopping out of the water and waddling toward the buckets, opening their mouths. "Okay, you can see they know it's lunchtime!"

I looked out at the crowd. There, with his back to me, looking at the Humboldts, was Jackson.

Jackson and a girl.

A girl I'd never seen before. An impossibly pretty African American girl, with a head full of tiny dreadlocks.

A girl who reached out, there in the dark, and took his hand.

"If you don't like eating fish, you wouldn't like to be a penguin!" I squeaked out, feeling Anya's eyes on me. "The keepers are feeding them anchoveta, little fish that live in the waters off the South American coast. Humboldts also eat squid and crustaceans."

Jackson leaned down and whispered in the girl's ear. I could feel heat rushing to my face. My mouth felt dry, and I could hardly keep going.

"They don't have to drink water, since they take in

seawater as they swallow their fish. But like all penguins, they have a special gland that removes the salt from their bodies."

That sick feeling that I had every day last year in the refectory, watching Jackson and Kim together after they hooked up, flooded through me. I couldn't take my eyes off him. Would he recognize my voice and turn around?

Had he recognized it already?

"Some fun facts about Humboldt penguins," I said, my hands shaking as I held the speech in front of me. "They can swim at speeds of up to thirty miles an hour, using their wings to propel them forward while steering with their webbed feet. After mating, the female lays two white eggs. Both mom and dad take turns sitting on them until they hatch, a real case of shared parenting!"

Jackson moved around behind the girl and put his arms around her, hugging her from the back.

I couldn't stand it anymore. I skipped the whole part I was supposed to say about the Humboldts' being endangered by commercial fishing and communicating by flipper waving. "Well," I said, speaking as fast as I could, "you can see they're nearly done with lunch! Thank you for visiting our Humboldt penguins today. And make sure to stop by the reticulated python feeding in the reptile house at four o'clock."

I stepped down from the footstool as fast as I could and started pushing the AV cart back toward the closet— but I was in such a rush I forgot to turn off the mike and unplug the equipment, so first the microphone let out a horrible screech, and then the electrical cord jerked and the rolling stand toppled over.

Anya jumped forward and braced it, and between the two of us we got it upright again. "Sorry, sorry," I muttered, bending down and pulling the cord out of the socket.

Standing up, I couldn't help looking in Jackson's direction again.

He was looking straight at me.

●

When the crowds cleared out and we had put the AV equipment away, Anya gave me a talking-to. Blah blah blah wasn't fully prepared, blah blah blah she knew I was nervous and it was my first time, blah blah blah maybe I needed another training session or should work another few hours for Lewis instead if I didn't like public speaking.

I barely listened to her.

Jackson was seeing someone. Behind Kim's back.

Even after what happened last year, I never thought he would do something like this. Kim swore to me that she and Jackson had never acted on their feelings until he and I had broken up, and there was comfort in the idea that they'd stuck to the rules. That I hadn't been a complete dupe. That I hadn't been kissing him and thinking I was going out with him when really he was with someone else.

That he hadn't been bareface lying to me.

I knew Jackson wasn't the person I'd thought he was when we were going out. But I'd always believed what Kim said: when they got together, they'd been blindsided by love into doing something that was out of character for both of them. And all that stuff that happened during the Spring Fling debacle could be explained if you think (like my dad does) that Jackson was torn and confused by his emotions.

But he wasn't torn and confused now. He was watching a penguin feeding. He had a girlfriend in Tokyo who had only left town four weeks earlier and who was coming back at winter break.

And he was out with someone else.

●

When I got home, I called Nora and Meghan and told them I wasn't going to Kyle's party.

Nora I had to lie to. I couldn't tell her about seeing Jackson in the zoo, or how I'd written him back after he wrote me that note.

I had never told her it was Jackson who invited me to Kyle's in the first place.

So I said I was having an attack of leprosy and had to stay home.

Meghan I told everything. She said there was no way she was going to the party without me and invited me over to sit in her hot tub instead. So we did that, getting cans of pop and looking out at the lake while we soaked. The air was chilly, and steam rose from the tub like a tropical mist.

I explained the whole Jackson scenario in gory detail. It was a relief to put it all into words. But as usual, Meghan's interpretation was woefully simple. "Forget it, Roo," she told me. "Jackson is nothing to you anymore, and Kim's nothing to you either. Just let it go."

But they weren't nothing to me. They were still huge, enormous somethings, even after all this time.

"In my Yoga Elective," Meghan went on, "we do all

this tension release. The idea is that you *surrender* to the pose, whatever stretchy position you're in, and release into it, letting go of all the stuff that's making it hurt."

"But don't you think if someone is doing something wrong to someone else, even someone you don't like, you should say something?" I asked, hiking myself up to sit on the edge of the tub.

"You should *stay out of it*," said Meghan, taking a drink of Sprite.

I slid back into the water and dunked my head.

●

Sunday, Nora came over. We watched *Hairspray* on video and she told me about Kyle's party. She went with Cricket. This was the news: Katarina scammed with Jackson's friend Matt. Ariel and Shiv seemed to be having some fight and Nora drove Ariel home. Cricket and Heidi spent most of their time flirting with some senior guys from the basketball team, stud-muffins we'd never noticed last year.

"Josh said something about my boobs," reported Nora, "and Noel stood up for me."

"Noel was there?"

"Noel always goes to parties, Roo. He *acts* like he doesn't like them, but he always goes. He knows all those guys from cross-country."

She had a point. "How did he stand up for you?"

"Told Josh to enter the twenty-first century or fuck off."

Score one for the Rescue Squad.

"Have you ever seen Noel dance?" Nora asked.

I hadn't.

"He's hilarious. None of the other guys would dare dance around like that. He told me his brother took him to these gay nightclubs last summer in New York City."

"Yeah, he told me that, too."

Part of me didn't like thinking of Nora and Noel hanging around together without me. But that is the sort of possessive jealous-lady thought I should probably stop having, so I kept quiet on that topic. "What did Josh say about your boobs?" I asked.

"Two things of beauty are a joy forever."[1]

I smiled. "You have to admit, that's a little bit funny."

"He's such an asshole," said Nora. "You'd think I'd have a snappy comeback by now, but I stand there like an idiot, wanting to hit someone."

"We should think of stuff to say. Like when guys say things to us on the streets or in the hall. So we're prepared."

"Genius!" cried Nora.

And that's how we ended up pulling out *The Boy Book,* which Nora hadn't even looked at since March, before the debacle, and starting a fresh page.

---

[1] It's a quote. We learned it in Brit Lit last year. John Keats, the Romantic poet, wrote: "A thing of beauty is a joy forever. / Its loveliness increases; it will never / Pass into nothingness."

9.

Clever Comebacks to Catcalls

Situation: You are walking down the hall, and someone tells you he's so ready for that jelly. Or you are strolling down the street and some construction worker on his lunch break says, "Come on, baby, lemme see you smile." What can you answer?

1. Join the twenty-first century.
2. Try to imagine how little I care.
3. Have you had your brain checked? I think the warranty has run out.
4. I can't get angry at you today. It's Be Kind to Animals Week.
5. Didn't I dissect you in Biology class?
6. Did you take your medication today?
7. I'll try smiling—if you try being smarter.
8. I'm curious, did your mother raise all of her children to be sexists, or did she single you out?

And some extras, for specific situations:

If he says, "If I could see you naked, I'd die happy," then you say, "If I could see you naked, I'd die laughing."

And if he says, "Hey, baby, what's your sign?" answer, "Do not enter."

And if he calls down the street as you ignore him, "Hey, baby, don't be rude!" reply, "I'm not being rude. You're just insignificant."

And if he says, "Can I see you sometime?" say, "How about never? Is never good for you?"

—written by me and Nora, after some serious Internet research.[1]
Approximate date: October of junior year.

It felt great to be friends with Nora again, even if there were subjects we couldn't discuss. Like I wanted to ask her if Kim and Jackson had maybe broken up, and how she felt that Cricket was spending most of her time with Katarina and Heidi and those guys. I wanted to tell her I saw Jackson at the zoo, and that he'd called to invite me to Kyle's party.

But it was safer not to.

The next week at school, though most of the boob comments had died down, Nora used comeback numbers four and five on Darcy Andrews and one of his cohorts, with excellent and pleasing results. And on Wednesday we went to the B&O with Meghan after sports practice and talked to Finn Murphy, who was waiting tables. We ate cake

---

[1] One of my favorite insults that we found, though it doesn't fit any of these scenarios, comes from Groucho Marx: "I've had a perfectly wonderful evening. But this wasn't it."

and drank espresso milk shakes, and I brought *The Boy Book* and we showed it to Meghan.

"Maybe I need to have a fling," mused Meghan, after reading the part about scamming. She sighed and rolled her eyeballs toward Finn, who was wiping down some tables on the other side of the café.

"What's going on with Bick?" I asked, since she had sort of brought it up.

"Aren't you two really serious?" put in Nora, wide-eyed.

"We're taking things one day at a time."

"Finn is cute," said Nora, checking out his backside as he bent over a dirty table.

"I don't know," mused Meghan. "Maybe if Bick and I did it, everything would go back to normal between us. He's coming home for Thanksgiving."

"You're not doing it?" Nora asked.

"They're just up to the nether regions," I informed her. "Or down to them. Whatever."

"You should *not* be doing it with someone who's on one-day-at-a-time status," said Nora decisively. "That's a recipe for disaster."

"I know, I know." Meghan looked thoughtful. "It's just that I want things to be how they were. You know, like last year. When life was easy."

"Uh-huh."

"It's like Bick's a different person now. Like Harvard is changing him."

I took a big bite of cake. "Last year," I told her, "you didn't have *us*."

●

Six major things happened in October.

119

ONE. I went with my mom for the appointment with the new, health-insurance-accepting shrink. It was in a clinic affiliated with a hospital, and the waiting room was filled with people who looked really shattered. One woman in her fifties was rocking back and forth, muttering about some chip the aliens had put in her brain. A guy with no neck was asleep and snoring, and a nervous lady in a dirty coat was touching a potted plant and staring at it like it might speak to her.

I had an appointment for four o'clock, and we got there early and filled out some forms. Then we sat.

The only magazine was about health care. There was a plastic coffee table, and a television was blaring at top volume up in a corner. The news was on: two abducted children and a hotel fire. I couldn't imagine how anyone could be expected to maintain any semblance of decent mental health if they had to watch that stuff before every therapy appointment.

Mom and I waited.

And waited.

I read my Chemistry textbook and highlighted key concepts while she watched TV. Now and then a doctor or therapist would call out someone's name.

Half the time, the person wasn't there.

A fatally thin woman came in and folded herself into a corner seat. The sleeping man woke up and wandered out of the room even though no one had called his name.

"Maybe we should just go," I whispered at 4:25. "I don't like it here."

"Not happening, Ruby."

"Please, Mom. I've been okay for a long time."

"You're judging this place on appearances," my mother snapped. "Besides, I already paid my copayment."

"But—"

"You never have an open mind. Is it too much for me to ask you to keep an open mind?"

I slumped back down in my seat.

We waited.

And waited.

And waited.

At 5:10, my mother stood up. "Come on, Roo. We're going."

"What?"

"This is disgusting," she announced, in a typical Elaine Oliver reversal-of-policy-when-it-suits-her. "The treatment here is disrespectful and we're wasting our time."

I grabbed my backpack.

●

TWO. A week later, went to see the shrink my dad's friend Greg uses.

Doctor Acorn, or Steven, as I was supposed to call him, was thin and dry. After talking to me and my mother for forty-five minutes, and listening to her tell him that I was antisocial and didn't seem to have friends anymore and never went anywhere and had panic attacks, he recommended that I start on Prozac and Ativan.[2]

---

[2] In case you don't know, Prozac is an antidepressant, and Ativan is an anti-anxiety drug. They can help people a lot. But Doctor Acorn was completely pill happy. I mean, he can hardly evaluate me from listening to my mother. The woman thinks I'm a lesbian.

"But I haven't had a panic thing in months," I said.

"That's how we want to keep it," he said. "Am I sensing some resistance here?"

"Yes."

"It's a good idea to get the baseline chemistry taken care of, then follow that up with the talk therapy."

"But I'm not antisocial," I said, turning to Mom. "I slept over at Meghan's house three nights ago."

"Compared to what she was before, she's antisocial," my mom said to Doctor Acorn. "Plus, there may be some sexual issues she wants to discuss with you. Right, Roo?"

"Mom!"

"Roo, you can be open with Steven. He's heard it all before."

There was no way I was going to tell Doctor Acorn about my scamming with Angelo—or anything else that was going on in my life. He was like a dried-up slice of apple, without any juice left inside, and he didn't seem like he was listening to me so much as telling me what he thought was wrong with me.

I laid it out for my mother as soon as we left. No Doctor Acorn. No way.

●

"What are we going to do?" she moaned, with her head in her hands, sitting at the dinner table later that night.

"Stop making me see a shrink," I yelled from my place on the couch.

"But it's good for you," my mother said.

"Mom. Vegetables are good for me. Sports activities. My job at the zoo is even good for me. But waiting for more than an hour with a bunch of madmen is not, and neither is taking drugs for problems I'm not even having."

"Wasn't Doctor Z good for you?" my father asked.

I didn't answer him.

●

THREE. Meghan called Bick on his cell and a girl answered.

"Um, this is Meghan, is Bick around?"

And the girl said, "Oh, yeah, Meghan! I've heard all about you. I'm Bick's friend Cecily."

"Oh. Hi."

"Hiya. Didn't he tell you about me?"

"No."

"The one from Maine, the one with the convertible?"

"Um, I don't think so."

"Bick went to get a drink—guys, do you know where Bick went?—and he left his cell on the table so I answered it. Oh my god, Holmes, you are so dead! Stop it! Oh my god, do you really go to Harvard?" Cecily was laughing, talking to some people around her, hardly even remembering she was on the phone.

Meghan hung up.

Bick didn't call her back until the next day.

●

FOUR. Noel, Meghan, Nora and I were supposed to go to the movies on a Saturday night. But Meghan's mom decided she had to stay home for dinner all of a sudden, and Nora's brother, Gideon, surprised her family by driving down from Evergreen State College, an hour or two away, so Nora wanted to stay and see him.

I picked up Noel in the Honda. His mom wouldn't

let him drive the Vespa at night. His house was a big Victorian-style place in Madrona, and when I went inside, Mr. and Mrs. DuBoise (his mom and stepdad that he's had for like fourteen years) were in the middle of a ginormous collaborative cooking project. The dining table was covered with vegetables chopped into tiny pieces, and Mrs. DuBoise had three open cookbooks stacked one on top of the other.

A couple of smaller DuBoises were running underfoot. Everything smelled like frying onions.

"We're glad to meet you, Ruby." The stepdad had a booming voice and was yelling over water running in the kitchen sink. "We've heard all about you."

"I was hoping my reputation hadn't preceded me," I said—which sounded like a joke, but which I really meant, given the suckiness of my reputation.

"Ha, ha!" the stepdad boomed. "All good, all good, I promise."

"Noel will be down in a minute," his mother said, wiping her hands on her apron. "He's doing something with hair gel."[3]

"No problem."

"Do you want a pop?"

"Nah. I'm good."

"What movie are you seeing?"

"Singin' in the Rain," I answered. "At that retro film place in the U District. They're doing an all-musical weekend, and my mom said this was the one to see."

---

[3] Hair gel.
   He was getting ready. To go somewhere.
   With *me*.

"You must be some girl, Ruby," laughed his mom, "if Noel is willing to go see a musical with you."[4]

"He made fun of us last week for renting *The Sound of Music*," added his stepdad. "He doesn't even like *My Fair Lady*. I mean, what's not to love about *My Fair Lady*?"

"You mean, besides the fact that it's completely sexist?" I asked.

"What?"

"It is. The man molds the woman into his ideal mate, changes everything about her—and she loves him for it. It completely bothers me. Shouldn't he like her for who she is? Because by the time he realizes he loves her, he's loving this shell of a person who has no sense of self."

Mrs. DuBoise laughed. "I can see why Noel likes you," she said. "I bet you give him a run for his money."

"Excuse them," said Noel, coming into the kitchen. "They've only just been let out of their cages."

"I'm sure we totally embarrassed you, honey," said his mother, blowing him a kiss. "Just thank your stars you weren't here to suffer through most of it."

"I suffered through enough," said Noel.

"Back by eleven!" boomed the stepdad as we went out the door.

"Don't forget your puffer!" yelled his mom.

We got in the Honda.

It had been an awful lot like picking him up for a date.

●

---

[4] Noel didn't want to go to this movie? When I'd invited him, he'd seemed completely cranked.

Singin' in the Rain was most excellent if you like movies where people burst into song and tap-dance. Which I do, though not as much as I like movies where people don't.

Afterward, we walked down one side of the Ave, which was filled with busy restaurants and boisterous college students, then back up the other side. There was a slight drizzle, like there usually is in Seattle, and the streets looked shiny in the lamplight.

When I asked, Noel talked about his asthma. He got a little touchy about it, though. Not like he was mad at me for asking, but like the whole thing just made him so angry that he hated to even have it mentioned.

To me it sounded like an annoying medical thing and not much else, but to Noel it was a box that he'd been shoved into. He was always trying to figure out how to push his way out.

He said that if his parents had their way he'd never go away for November Week, and he had to fight with them about it every year. How when he'd gone to New York City they'd given his brother Claude strict instructions about exactly when he should be taking his meds, as if they didn't trust him to do it himself. How they were always yelling out the door that he bring his puffer or pop his anti-inflammatories.

He didn't want people to know he had asthma, he said. If people knew, it would be like walking around with a sign on his back that said "Defective Goods," and he wasn't sure what made him drag me into the bushes that first day of school, because he never showed people his inhaler. Aside from the school nurse and the cross-country coach, both of whom *had* to know, I was the only one.

"Why me?" I asked.

"I don't have that many friends."

I socked him on the arm. "You're golden, Noel. You get invited to parties all the time. You could eat lunch with anyone you want."

"True enough. But I don't have them over to meet the folks like you did today. I'm not close to any of them."

"Oh." I hadn't thought of it like that.

"I've told you, the Tate Universe isn't quite my thing."

"And I am?" I said it sarcastically, and his answer surprised me:

"Yes," said Noel. "You are my thing."

Abruptly, he stopped walking. I stopped a few steps ahead and turned back to wait for him. I thought he was going to take my hand and kiss me,

and I thought that I wanted him to.

I thought, Oh, we're not friends, we're in love.

And then a pile of college students poured out of a bar next to where we were standing, laughing with their arms around each other, singing "Louie Louie."

Noel started walking again and began talking about frat rock as a genre.[5] So I asked, who were the Knack and

[5] Frat rock: Big, loud party music that is not disco or hip-hop or R&B. Music that you kind of have to like, even if you think it's dumb. Have you seen the movie *Animal House*? Like that. But it transcends time period. Some examples: "Louie Louie." "Shout." "Addicted to Love." "Whip It." "Wild Thing." "Old Time Rock 'n' Roll." "My Sharona." "Centerfold." "Our House." "Come On Eileen." "Gloria." "Mama Told Me (Not to Come)." "I Want Candy."

This list compiled by me and Noel, with additions from a later consultation with my dad.

why were they called that? Because I had seen something about them on "Behind the Music."

For my edification, Noel sang "My Sharona" in such a loud voice that everyone looked at us like we were insane as we walked up the Ave. Then we both sang "Wild thing . . . Dow dow dow NOW . . . I think I love you . . . Dow dow dow NOW . . . but I wanna knoooow for sure . . ."

We got in the Honda and went on discussing subjects generally related to frat rock (including the movie *The Blues Brothers,* the death of John Belushi, and old *Saturday Night Live* episodes we'd seen), and suddenly, we were in front of his house.

I stopped the car. He hopped out.

And I drove myself home.

The next day, nothing was sexy or romantic between us. It was all back to normal.

FIVE. In French Cinq (level five), we had to act out dramatic scenes from *Cyrano de Bergerac* and I was forced to be partners with Cricket.

Heidi and Ariel were in class with us too, but they partnered with each other, and Cricket was left with no one. We'd had an assignment like this once earlier in the term, and Cricket had partnered with a sophomore named Sophie, while I had partnered with Hutch.[6] But Hutch was absent, and Sophie had since made friends with another girl in the class, so Cricket got stuck with me.

---

[6] Thus completely cementing my leper status, but actually beneficial to me in the grade department because Hutch is très good at Français and actually sounds Frenchie when he says stuff.

We hadn't spoken for months, but she had never talked any crap about me that I could hear, and she never bothered Nora for refriending me. She just pretended I didn't exist.

After Madame Long split us up into partners, Cricket dragged her backpack across the room to where I was sitting.

"Hi."

"Hi."

"Do you want to be Roxane or Cyrano?"

"You can be Cyrano," I said. "You are the summer drama camp goddess. You'll do it better."

I was so mad at her and I wanted her to like me again, if that makes any sense.

Like, I didn't think she was such a good person anymore, and she didn't think I was such a good person anymore, but she had always made me laugh and I missed her.

"Okay," Cricket said.

So we read through the scene, with everyone else reading through scenes all around us, and I thought, God, each second of this is torture because we're so mad at each other, and also, This is kind of fun and maybe we'll be friends again.

We practiced until the end of the period. When Madame Long told us to stop, Cricket immediately stood up and put her book in her backpack. "Later," she said—and I thought, Really? Does she mean later, as in she'll see me later, she'll talk to me later? although I knew it was just a phrase.

I left class slowly, feeling relieved to at least have talked to Cricket after all this time, and stupidly hopeful.

Cricket was standing in the hall with Ariel and Heidi, who had come out of French across the way. As I walked past them, I waved.

"Heya," said Heidi.

"God, she is so annoying," Cricket complained, loud enough for me to hear.

And I thought, Annoying? What did I do?

I did nothing; we just read the scene.

I understand if she thinks I'm a bad person. But since when am I annoying?

Why would she think that?

Heidi elbowed Cricket in the ribs. "She can hear you," she whispered.

"Fine," said Cricket, even louder. "She should know how annoying she is."

"Try to imagine how little I care," I lied.

●

SIX. I finally called Angelo. Two weeks after going to the movies with Noel, and three weeks after he first gave me his cell number.

It wasn't that I didn't want to call before. It was more that I knew it would be awkward when I did, because Angelo and I hadn't figured out how to talk to each other yet.

And maybe we never would.

Besides which, I couldn't sort out my feelings.

I liked him. He had nice fat lips and was a camp counselor and was funny with his dogs and was practically a medalist at boob groping. But there were complicating factors. Five, to be precise.

1. Our moms were friends.
2. I'd lied to Jackson about Angelo being my boyfriend.
3. I was jealous of the zoo girl being with Jackson.[7]
4. I kept thinking about those two times with me and Noel when I thought he might kiss me.[8]
5. The physical side with Angelo had progressed pretty far, pretty fast. You know, straight to the groping on day one. And though that whole part of it was my idea, I'd never gone any farther than the upper regions. Not even with Jackson. I had no idea what Angelo would be expecting on our third encounter, but it would almost certainly get horizontal.

●

Still, I wanted to kiss him again. I mean, I had gone months kissing no one after the Spring Fling debacle, but now that I had remembered what it was like, I was interested. And I thought, Why are you overanalyzing and making yourself miserable? Angelo is a good guy. You like each other at least enough to go hang out for an evening. It's not marriage. It's one date. So just call him. Go out with him. See what happens.

He answered on the second ring. *"Hola."*

"Hi, it's Ruby," I said.

---

[7] I am deranged, I know. But that is how I felt.

[8] Because if this was a film of my life, that would be the plot. Noel would turn out to be the hero.

Movies where a guy and a girl are just good friends, and one of them likes

"Oh, sorry," he laughed. "I thought you were going to be somebody else."

"No. Just me," I said. And went right to the point. "Do you wanna, um, hang out sometime?"

"What, like, sometime soon?"

"Yeah, that's what I was thinking."

There was an awkward pause. "Roo, I, um . . ."

"What?"

"You never called . . ."

"I'm sorry. I've just been busy."

". . . so I figured you weren't into it."

"Oh."

"I mean, that's okay. You don't have to be into it if you don't feel it. You should do what's right for you."

"Um-hm."

"I mean, I started seeing someone," he said. "When you didn't call. This girl at my school. And I–I don't want to step out on her."

Of course. "No, no," I said. "I wasn't asking you that."

"It was just . . . you didn't call. And you told me not to call *you,* which is why I didn't."

"You're completely right," I answered. "That is what I said."

Here was Angelo, who wouldn't step out on a girl he'd only been seeing for two weeks. A guy who, though

somebody else, but at the end they finally realize they love each other with a mad passion: *Clueless. The Sure Thing. Can't Hardly Wait. Some Kind of Wonderful. When Harry Met Sally. The Wedding Singer. Emma. Sabrina. Win a Date with Tad Hamilton.*

certainly not skilled in the telephone department, appeared to be straightforward and honest.

A cute guy who liked me and I liked him and maybe we could have had a thing together.

And I had ruined it.

I got off the phone as quickly as I could.

10.

Why You Want the Guy You Can't Have: Inadequate Analysis of a Disturbing Psychological Trend

Fact: I like Angelo more now that I can't have him.[1]

How could I have been so stupid, not to call? I am full of regret.

Angelo, being a mentally stable type of person, stopped liking me once he figured I was unavailable. But me, no. My brain and heart do the opposite of what would be in their best interests.

Why do we want what we can't have? Are we conditioned to feel that way by toxic advertising images, social pressures and bad stuff that happens to us? And is there anything we can do to change the situation?

Because I know that, neurotic as I am, I am not alone. Cricket

---

[1] And I liked Jackson more too—ever since I'd seen him with the zoo girl. Well, *liked* isn't the right word. But I hated him and wanted him to want me instead of her. But I couldn't put that in *The Boy Book,* because Nora would probably read the entry.

crushed on Billy Alexander all last year, and it started the same week he began seeing Molly.[2] And Ariel started liking Shiv when he went out with that freshman.

A guy becomes instantly more desirable when he is with someone else. And that is bad. Because you can't have him. And also because it's stupid and kind of sick.

On one hand, it makes sense: if everyone says the new peanut butter ice cream is excellent, you'd probably want to try it, even if peanut butter isn't usually your thing, right? You might not like it once you'd tried it, but you would want to see what the hype was all about. And you certainly wouldn't have gotten interested in it if someone else hadn't pointed out how good it was.

On the other hand, it's like we're three years old. You don't want that scruffy old teddy bear until your friend takes it and starts having a good time with it. Then suddenly it's the cutest bear you've ever seen, and you want to get it away from her.

Ag.

Shouldn't we be past that by now, and all be falling in love or making out with people who are actually available?

Why are we like this? A few possible theories:

1. Our dads were always going off to work or reading the newspaper when we were little, so now our vision of the ideal man is one who isn't interested in us. (Very Freudian.)
2. Our dads were in love with our moms, so everyone from infancy (except maybe people raised by single parents or two moms) has this thing where the man they love the best is in love with someone else. (Even more Freudian. Ag. We can stop going there now.)

---

[2] And Kim started liking Jackson when he was with me. Also left out of *The Boy Book* entry to avoid fighting with Nora.

3. The point of a lot of advertising, as Mr. Wallace explained to us last year in American History & Politics, is to spark desire by creating a sense of inadequacy. Like, we look at some fashion model in a magazine and think, Whoa, I'm ugly and oddly plump next to her. I suck. She's great. What can I buy to make myself suck less? Oh, that eye shadow she's modeling. So the magazine photo makes us feel like crap and then we want something. And we're used to that, because ads are such a huge part of our society. So then when a guy makes us feel bad (by going out with someone else or rejecting us), we respond by wanting something (him).

4. We're slaves to whatever's popular. And if a guy has a girlfriend, he's more popular (pretty much) than any guy who's free.

5. We are actually scared to have real live boyfriends that we'd have to be all intimate with, so it's safer to like someone we can't have.

6. Then again, maybe it's just true that the cute guys are always taken and I should stop analyzing so much.

Whatever the reason, liking a guy who's already taken is a recipe for horror. But how to stop liking a person you like? Even if you know your psychotic, messed-up heart is only playing tricks on you?

Practically impossible.

—from *The Boy Book*, written by me, Ruby Oliver. Approximate date: late October, junior year.

When I showed the entry to Meghan at the B&O a couple of days later, she reached into her book bag and pulled out a pen. "Is it okay if I add something?"

"Sure," I said, though it had never occurred to me

she'd want to. Partly because, well, she wasn't Cricket or Nora or Kim. And partly because she's not the analytical type. But she wrote for a long time, then handed it back to me. I read:

Another thing that's toxic in this whole trend of people wanting what they can't have is that it leads to evil, manipulative games. Like girls who try to make their boyfriends jealous because then the boys will like the girls even *more* when they think said girls want somebody else. Or girls who lie to guys, saying they have a boyfriend when they don't. Or guys who ignore their girlfriends in public, because they think that seeming uninterested will make the girl actually more devoted.

All of which sometimes works.

But then, everyone is fake, and half of them have had their feelings hurt.

Maybe the thing to do is to refuse to play those games, even if you are tempted. Part of me wants to find someone to have a fling with in order to make Bick start paying attention. Because now he hardly seems to know I exist—and I think about him all the time.

Which is awful.

But if he thought I *wasn't* thinking about him, and I was thinking of someone else instead, I bet he'd think of *me*.

But I shouldn't go having flings I don't want to have in order to make my boyfriend notice me. And I shouldn't pretend that I don't like him so he'll come crawling back. Because it's creepy and stupid.

It would be better to stop liking him for real. Then I'd be a lot happier.

—written by Meghan. Approximate date: late October, junior year.

"Wow," I said. "I didn't know you were still that shattered about this whole thing."

Meghan nodded.

"Are you gonna break up with him?"

"No."

"Why not?"

"It was only when I wrote that just now that I even thought I'd be happier if I *didn't* love Bick."

"Oh."

"But the problem is, I do. I can't break up with someone I want to be with."

"You can't?"

"How can I walk away from him when I want him so much? Doesn't that seem like giving up on love?"

I felt like telling her she should dump him. He made her feel like crap and she'd be better off without him. But I knew I'd never have walked away from Jackson if he hadn't broken with me. Things had already been weird between us for months before the debacle. Little events (or nonevents) shattered me, like when I baked him black-bottom cupcakes and he barely even noticed. Or when he didn't buy me a Christmas present. Or didn't ask me to the Spring Fling until really late. Or the whole Valentine's Day flower horror.

For pretty long, before we broke up, being with Jackson had made me feel more bad than good.

But I never would have left.

"I know what you mean," I told Meghan.

"I'd be happier if I didn't like him," she said again, like she was trying out the sound of it.

●

I dialed Angelo's cell twice one day, having this idea that if I told him I was thinking about him all the time, and reminded him what it was like that night in the Honda,

and told him that I wanted him,

he'd break up with the other girl.

But he didn't even pick up. I didn't leave a message.

He probably looked at his cell to see who had called, and he didn't ring me back.

●

Thursday night before November Week was Halloween. My parents were going to the same big party they go to each year, and they had spent the whole afternoon getting ready.

Mom was going as Frida Kahlo, the artist, and had drawn her eyebrows together, put on nearly black lipstick and found some Mexican peasant clothing. She was forcing my dad to be Salvador Dalí, my favorite painter, who had an insane mustache. She glued it on his lip and squeezed him into a red velvet coat, a yellow shirt and a long-haired wig.

There was a party at Jackson's friend Matt's, but I don't need to tell you I wasn't going. Meghan came over and we watched *The Ring*, *The Others* and half of *The Exorcist* before we got too scared and had to turn on all the lights and eat Popsicles to de-freak ourselves.

●

The Friday before November Week, Nora pulled me aside when she saw me in the refectory. "Kim is coming home," she whispered. "Her flight gets in this morning."

"What?" I was shocked.

"She doesn't like the exchange program."

"Why not?"

"Her host family is mean to her. She's been really homesick."

Oh.

I had figured that Kim, who had traveled all over the world with her parents on vacation, was having a great time in Japan. It had never occurred to me that she was doing anything but having glamorous, independent adventures. "How did you find out?"

"E-mail. But here's what I have to tell you. Please don't be mad."

"What?"[3]

"Like two weeks ago, before she told me she was coming home, Kim asked me what I was doing for November Week. So I told her."

"And?"

"And I said it sounded cool, and Mr. Wallace was leading it, and there was a swimming pool and a sauna. But I didn't tell her it was you and me and Noel."

"You lied?" Nora never lies.

"I left that part out. About you and me being friends again. I didn't want things to get complicated."

"So?"

Nora twisted a curl on one of her fingers but didn't answer.

---

[3] I hate it when people say "Please don't be mad." Because you're almost always *going* to be mad at whatever they've done, and even if you aren't mad about that, you feel mad anyway, because even before telling you about it they have (1) implied that you're the kind of person who gets mad about all kinds of things unreasonably, and (2) attempted to squelch your self-expression.

"She's coming with us." My voice sounded heavy in my own ears.

"I'm so sorry," said Nora. "I had no idea that's why she was asking. She was in Tokyo!"

"No, there was no way you could know."

"It turns out Jackson's doing rafting, which is completely full. And she probably knew Cricket was doing Mount Saint Helens, but Cricket's been so deep in Katarina-Heidi Land, I think Kim decided she'd rather pick Canoe Island."

"Did you tell her I was going?"

Nora shook her head. "I was so shocked when I got her e-mail, I didn't reply."

"But Cricket might have told her."

"Yeah, maybe. Cricket knows I'm going with you."

The whole thing was a certain horror.

"Maybe I can get out of it," I said. "Maybe my parents can get a refund."

"Maybe," she said. "But you were so cranked to go."

"Not anymore."

"I'm sorry." Nora bit her thumbnail.

"I'm going to pull out and do that public school greening project."

"Really, really sorry," said Nora.

"Me too," I said.

●

But when I told Noel I was pulling out, he said, Don't. "You can't let fear run you."

And then I told Meghan, and she said, Don't. "Kim is nothing to you. Remember?"

"We'll miss you," said Mr. Wallace. "Are you sure you don't want to reconsider? No one's going to take your spot at this late date. You can show up for the ferry tomorrow morning if you change your mind."

I called Nora that afternoon after my zoo job. "If Kim signed up for Canoe Island knowing I was going," I said, "that's awful."

"How so?"

"Because she can't actually *want* to be there if I'm there. It's obvious the whole thing will be a debacle. She's forcing me out."

"I don't think Kim would do that. She probably doesn't know."

"I bet she does."

"She's not evil, Roo. You two just don't get along anymore."

"I feel like she's going to come back from Tokyo and steal the only three friends I have," I said. "I'm going to end up with no one."

"I never stopped being friends with her," said Nora. "You know that. And I don't want to be in the middle. Can't everyone just be polite?" Nora is always one for people getting along. She likes life to be orderly.

"I doubt it," I said. "Are you going to tell her I'm going?"

"Not if you're staying home and doing the greening project."

"But if she's as innocent as you think," I said, "she'll pull out when she hears I'll be there."

"Roo, please, please, please don't get me more in the middle of this than I already am."

I sighed. Nora was right.

"Okay," I said. "Sorry."

"So are you going?"

"Yes," I answered, surprising myself. "I am."

11.

The Kaptain Is In

Dear Kaptain Kangaroo,

I gave a boy named Billy my number at a party after he kissed me. So why didn't he call?

Answer: Don't angst, he'll call.

Dear Kaptain Kangaroo,

I think he should call three days after kissing me and getting my number. That's only polite, plus I read it somewhere online. And now it's been two weeks. So if he does call, what should I say?

Answer: Tell him you're busy and you'll call him back. And then don't. That's the best he deserves.

Dear Kaptain,

But I want to talk to him!

Answer: You shouldn't, though.

But Kaptain, if he calls me, doesn't he like me? Which means I should
talk to him. Blowing him off isn't going to get me anywhere.
Answer: Sweetie, he's not going to call. If he was going to, he'd have
called already!

But Kaptain, you said he'd call!
Answer: Sometimes the Kaptain tells little white lies to make her
friends feel better. Sorry. You'd better forget him.

—questions by me, answers by Kim. Approximate date: summer
after freshman year.

We had invented Kaptain Kangaroo[1] as *The Boy Book* advice columnist at the start of ninth grade. Most of the Kaptain's columns degenerate from the advice format into just notes. Sometimes Kim and I would hand the book back and forth in school, so the exchange lasted a whole day. Other times, we'd sit side by side watching a movie on TV at her house, making entries during the boring parts.

We took turns being Kaptain.

The above entry was written during an insane two weeks in the summer when this boy I kissed at a toga party never called. I couldn't believe that I could kiss someone

---

[1] Captain Kangaroo was this old guy on children's television who my dad is always talking about. Kangaroo comes from me (Roo) and Kim (Kanga). And "The Kaptain Is In" comes from those Peanuts cartoons where Lucy is the shrink and she has a sign that says "The Doctor Is In." (Kim has a huge stack of *Peanuts* books, and we used to read them all the time when we were younger.) So that's how we thought of it.

and it would seem like the start of something, and he'd ask for my number, and then I'd never see him again. It didn't seem possible.[2] Even the first guy I kissed, a guy at camp who was completely gross, was around for the last ten days of camp, so it wasn't like a kiss-and-disappear.

Anyway, packing for Canoe Island was boring, and my mind was spinning in a frenzy of nerves, so I pulled out *The Boy Book* and paged through it, reading old entries and thinking about me and Kim and how we used to be.

Best friends.

It seemed like it would last forever back then.

As I was reading, I came across an entry way at the back of the book where all the rest of the pages were blank. The questions were in Nora's handwriting, and the answers were in Cricket's—and I remembered that back in February I had left the book at Nora's house for several weeks before retrieving it.

Dear Kaptain Kangaroo,
My friend's boyfriend is annoying and I wish she'd break up
with him. What should I do?
Answer: Suck it up, baby. All guys are annoying sometimes.
Even most of the time. Unless you're going out with them.

---

2 Movies where the heroine meets a guy who is funny and cute and kisses her— but then she never lays eyes on him ever again: none.

So of course I thought Billy would eventually call, or we'd run into each other and he'd have an explanation, or something. Because on some level, even though it never turns out to be true, and even though I should know better, I still expect life to be like the movies.

Dear Kaptain Kangaroo,

What if he's mean to her?

Answer: Different situation. If he puts her down, makes her do sex things she doesn't like, or does any of those horrors you read about in magazines, you're entitled to tell your friend he sucks.

Dear Kaptain,

But what if he's not tangibly mean, he just makes her feel terrible with all kinds of manipulative weirdness?

Answer: Are you talking about the whole Valentine's Day thing?

Nora: And the cupcakes and how he talked to Heidi all night at Kyle's party in December and a million other small horrors.

Cricket: Like how he blew her off for that basketball game and then made her feel guilty for being mad.

Nora: Exactly.

Cricket: I know. It sucks so much. The Kaptain has no answer. You've really stumped her this time.

They were writing about me and Jackson, of course.

But I had never had any clue they thought *that* about the stuff that had been going on. I'd always thought they *liked* Jackson, and considered me lucky to have him.

And now it turned out they thought he treated me badly.

And I knew it was true. But it was different to see it written down by people on the outside.

Part of me went right into Jackson-girlfriend mode, even though I hadn't been his girlfriend for almost half a year, thinking: They don't know him. They don't know how he is when he's alone with me. How it is when we kiss. What it's like when we hang out at his house, the way he writes me all those funny notes, the way he laughs at my jokes.

And another part of me was thinking:

I am better off without him.

I am better off without him.

I am really, truly better off without him.

Which I had never thought before.

●

Saturday morning at dawn, we all had to meet at a ferry dock two hours north in Anacortes, where a charter boat was taking us to Canoe Island. My dad drove me. My hands were shaking so badly whenever I thought of seeing Kim again that I started to wish I had some of the pills Doctor Acorn had been so cranked about.

As we drove, I tried to do a therapy assignment Doctor Z had given me awhile back, which was to acknowledge to myself precisely what I feared, rather than letting it be vague.

Ruby's List of Canoe Island Paranoias:

1. *Kim will repeat her version of the Spring Fling debacle to anyone and everyone who doesn't already know it, and any small bit of the Canoe Island contingency who were friendly to me will turn cold and mean.*

2. *Once Kim has reminded the boys what a slut I supposedly am, they will harass me and the whole trip will be one long siege of dick photography–type jokes.*[3]
3. *Kim will haze me in some way, like pouring soup on my sleeping bag, throwing out my swimsuit or putting garbage in my duffel bag.*
4. *Kim and I will get in some completely embarrassing public argument.*
5. *Kim will make Nora stop talking to me.*
6. *And Noel, too.*

As my dad sped the Honda along the freeway, I massaged my own hands (a therapy relaxation technique) and reminded myself:

Kim is not the devil. She's a person.

A person you used to love.

Her whole agenda in life is not to torture you. She probably never even thinks about you.

And please. She's not going to pour soup on your sleeping bag. This is eleventh grade.

You survived May and June sophomore year and the world didn't come to an end. The two of you saw each other every day in school. So much time has passed since then that seeing her shouldn't be any big thing.

So why are you freaking out?

---

[3] True, I was completely ready to say "Didn't I dissect you in Biology class?"—but I'd rather it didn't happen in the first place.

Dear Kaptain,

I am guilty. Because of Jackson and the notes and the hiking up my skirt to show off my legs.

And I know he's stepping out on her.

And Kaptain, in June of sophomore year I had nothing left to lose.

But now I have Nora and Noel. If they ditch me, all I'll have is Meghan.

Answer: What's done is done (with Jackson). What you know about the stepping out is none of your business anyway. And if Noel and Nora are really your friends, you won't lose them. And if you lose them, then you don't want that kind of friend anyway.

But Kaptain . . .

Answer: What now?

Kaptain, I'm just getting more and more freaked out the more I think of all this stuff.

Answer: You're being completely irrational.

Me: It's how I feel.

The Kaptain in my head didn't reply.

I breathed as deeply as I could and watched the buildings fly by outside the car window.

●

When we arrived, Kim wasn't there yet. The ferry dock was bustling. The air was damp, and seagulls were wandering around looking for snacks. Kids were saying goodbye to their parents, sleeping bags and suitcases piled around them.

Here's who was there:

Varsha and Spencer from swim team, plus Spencer's boyfriend (Imari, captain of the boys' team),

Nora and Noel,

three senior boys who were very studious and hung around together all the time (Kieran, Mason and Grady),

two quiet senior girls I'd never talked to (Mei and Sierra),

Courtney, a senior who used to go out with Jackson when they were ninth graders, and two of her friends (who were basically interchangeable),

a posse of giggling sophomores,

Mrs. Glass,

Mr. Wallace

and Hutch.[4]

Ag, Hutch!

He had never told me he was going.

Except Varsha, Wallace, Imari and Mei, everyone was white. Except for Hutch and Noel, everyone was wholesome. They were all wearing jeans and plaid jackets or chambray shirts–typical Tate outdoor activity clothes. They looked like they'd stepped out of some Northwest outerwear catalog. Even Noel had on a dark blue chambray, and Hutch was wearing new-looking hiking boots, though it's true he sported his usual Iron Maiden biker jacket.

---

[4] Most of these people don't end up being that important to the story I'm telling you. They were there on Canoe Island, and I talked philosophy with them and we cooked meals together, and they were nice enough—but you don't need to remember who everyone is. I'm just giving you the lay of the land.

I was wearing a vintage skirt and a beaded sweater, with fishnet stockings and combat boots.

Wrong, wrong, wrong.

My dad helped me unload my duffel, plus a sleeping bag we borrowed from a friend of his. I was supernervous and shivering, so I rooted around and found my jacket.

Nora came over (she's always great with parents) and said, "Hi, Mr. Oliver," and Noel said hello too. It was the first time he'd met my dad. Hutch held back, but Kevin Oliver was so cranked he leaped over a pile of suitcases and squeezed his shoulders.

"John!" he bellowed. "You're doing this Canoe Island, then?"

"Yeah."

"I thought for sure you'd do the greening project at the public school."

Hutch shrugged. "I wanted to go somewhere."

My dad nodded knowingly. "Anything to get out of the house at your age. I remember those days."

"Something like that."

"Well. Have fun canoeing."

"We're not canoeing, Dad," I reminded him. "We're reading philosophy."

"Same difference," my dad said, laughing loudly at his lame joke. "Okay. I'm gonna motor. Rock on, John! Keep an eye on Ruby for me!"

"Sure, man," said Hutch, looking at the ground with a smile snaking across his lips.

Having thoroughly humiliated me by making heavy metal devil-horn hand signals at Hutch while the other fathers patted their kids on the back and shook hands with each other, my dad hugged me goodbye, told me he loved me and hoped I would bond productively with my peer group, and left—right as the Yamamotos' Mercedes pulled up to the dock.

Kim got out, and Nora squealed and ran straight to her.

So that was how it was going to be.

●

Kim was jumping up and down. She'd had her hair cut into a very short bob. Tokyo chic.

She and Nora were hugging and checking each other out, the way girls do. I could hear them. "You look amazing, I can't believe your hair!"

Kim was rounder, more filled out, than when I'd seen her at the end of the school year last June. She was wearing her favorite old khaki jacket, but her sneakers looked futuristically Japanese.

"I'm so glad to be back. God, I was so miserable."

"Did you see Cricket last night? She said she was driving over, but my mom made me have family dinner, so I couldn't come."

"Yeah, she came out to Chez Shea with me and Jackson."

"I'm so jealous."

"Then we went to the B&O with Katarina and Ariel. We tried to call your cell at like nine-thirty but you didn't pick up."

"I forgot to charge it. Did you get my e-mail?"

"No, I never checked."

"You didn't get it?"

"No, I told you. Did you bring a swimsuit?"

And blah blah blah.

The Doctors Yamamoto, both of them, were unloading Kim's stuff from the Mercedes.

"Let's go buy chocolate," I said suddenly, thinking Noel was behind me. But it was Hutch, still standing there.

"Okay," he answered, checking his jacket pocket for his wallet.

So we left the dock and ran across the street to a little general store, where I spent money on caramel bars and jelly candies and mini Toblerones.

Hutch said he wasn't supposed to have actual chocolate because the dermatologist had told him it was bad for his skin, and he did have very bad skin—he'd had it for years at that point—but it had never occurred to me he was trying to do anything about it.

It had just seemed like part of him.

And, horrible to say, like it was somehow his fault.

Which is obviously wrong when you write it down, but which is still the kind of thought that can lurk in the back of your head when you don't really know someone.

So Hutch bought red licorice and sour straws and three rolls of hard candy. And we both got pop.

It was nice getting junk food at seven-thirty in the morning with no parents to tell you no.

●

The ferry was leaving. We all scrambled to get our stuff loaded on, then lined up so Mrs. Glass could check everyone off a list.

When it became absolutely necessary, Kim looked me in the eye and smiled a tight smile. "Hello, Ruby."

"Hi."

"How are you?"

"Good."

"That's nice."

Then she clutched the arm of one of the sophomore girls and started asking her about the crew team. As if I didn't exist.

Once the boat pulled onto the water, Hutch sat inside on a plastic yellow chair and jacked himself into his iPod. Kim and Nora and the sophomores went out on the deck.

Noel had been adopted by Courtney and her set of senior girls, who clearly judged Kieran, Mason and Grady too geeky to bother with. So I was alone. I pulled out a mystery novel and a Toblerone, found a seat near a window and started to read.

Forty-five minutes later, I went to the bathroom. It was painted yellow and had bits of stray toilet paper all over. Nora was in there, sitting on the gross floor.

She had been crying.

"What's wrong?" I was still pissed about how she'd ditched me for Kim at the terminal.

"Nothing. It's fine."

"Come on."

Nora wiped her nose.

"Kim didn't know you were coming. She's mad at me because I didn't tell her."

"I thought you were going to."

"I couldn't deal with calling her about it, so I sent her an e-mail. But she never got it." Nora put her hands over her face. "So now she's mad, and you know how she gets. She really yelled at me."

"Oh my God."

"Yeah. She made it sound like I had done this horrible

thing, being friends with you again without even checking with her or telling her. And she said, like, that I set her up, letting her come."

"You weren't setting her up."

"I know. But I didn't tell her, either." She started sobbing.

I didn't want to act like it was all okay, because it wasn't. It just wasn't.

So I gave Nora some jelly candies and the two of us sat there together, on that nasty floor, until the boat docked.

156

The island was awesome. Even with all that was going on, I was cranked to see the place. We were staying in a lodge that had rooms full of bunk beds, a big kitchen and a dining room with a view of the water, two saunas and a swimming pool. The teachers let us wander around and get settled, and once I'd dumped my stuff on a bunk bed I went out into the woods. There were broad paths running off in several directions, and I walked a ways on one, by myself.

It was peaceful. So peaceful that I could even imagine the trip would be civil and possibly fun. Kim would smile tightly at me, like she had on line for the boat ride, and we'd essentially ignore each other.

I'd spend the week with my friends, and nothing horrible would happen.

Peace would reign. Life would be sweet and easy.

Of course, I was wrong.

Canoe Island worked like this. In the mornings, we got up and straggled to breakfast and fended for ourselves. Glass cooked up scrambled eggs or pancakes if people got there by eight, but if you slept late you could eat peanut butter toast or something like that. There was a stack of Xeroxes on the breakfast table, and you were supposed to take one and read it before ten a.m. One day it was a section from Plato's *Republic* about a cave; another day it was from a book called *The Wretched of the Earth,* by Frantz Fanon; and another, a bit from *Zen and the Art of Motorcycle Maintenance,* by Robert Pirsig. Different kinds of readings, all chosen to make you think.

Then we'd have a group discussion for an hour and a half, led by Glass and Wallace. I didn't love the readings, but they were both so cranked over everything that the conversations were pretty interesting. Kim always sat off to one side, away from where I was.

Then we broke for lunch, which was sandwiches, and always un-vegetarian, so I ended up eating peanut butter again most days. Nora and Noel and I hung with Varsha and Spencer and Imari, and Kim stayed mainly with the senior girls. Hutch joined us sometimes, but overall he kept to himself.

After lunch, Glass offered a meditation session for an hour, which I did a couple of times. It was voluntary. You sat cross-legged on a mat in the big dining room and tried to think of nothing.

Which was impossible.

I'd think I was thinking of nothing, and then these thoughts would like attack my brain. About Angelo, and whether there was any hope for us. About Jackson, and how he was stepping out on Kim and she didn't know it. About Doctor Z, and how I kind of missed her.

Hutch fell asleep once and snored. I gave him a nudge

to wake him up, and Courtney and her friends laughed. "Shut up," I said.

And they did.

In the afternoon, we were free to swim, go in the sauna or explore the landscape. We were supposed to be thinking over the philosophical readings and connecting to the natural world. But mainly we checked each other out in our bathing suits or walked through the woods, talking about TV shows and fashion and stuff.

There turned out to be one other house on the island, I guess belonging to the owners, and it was a pretty big hike up a hill to get to it. Once you got there, though, they had three llamas in a big pen.

Llamas!

Varsha, Spencer and Nora, who were with me when I discovered them, were nervous. But I had dealt with Laverne and Shirley at the zoo, so I went right up and patted the white one on the neck. He nosed my fingers, hoping for treats.

"Are you sure you should pet that thing?" asked Varsha.

"Don't they spit?" muttered Spencer, hanging back.

"They're really soft," I said. "They won't spit unless you scare them. Come try."

Nora held out her hand shyly, but she yanked it back when the llama snorted. Varsha and Spencer kept a safe distance.

I scratched the soft fur, and whispered some llama compliments such as what a fine-lookin' specimen he was, what nice clean hooves he had, and so forth. And I felt, for the first time in a while, like I was good at something.

Something other people weren't good at.

Those of us on the swim team (Varsha, Spencer, Imari and me) worked out with Mr. Wallace in the later afternoons, though the pool was hardly long enough to build up any speed and it was harsh cold when we got out of the water. I worked on my flip turns, which have always been slow.

Then people were assigned to cook dinner, and other people were given jobs like making the Xeroxes for the next day or tidying up the central living area, and we did that until it was time to eat.

In the evenings, Wallace and Glass put movies on the DVD player. They said they picked films that were meant to spur our thinking on the issues we'd been talking about in the mornings, and also that they felt were just good for us to see, since we all probably watched lots of movies that were complete crap.[5]

We saw *Badlands, Brazil, Dr. Strangelove, Citizen Kane, The Piano, Do the Right Thing* and *One Flew over the Cuckoo's Nest*.

And you know what? I was the only one who'd seen them all before.

---

[5] Okay, they didn't say complete crap. They said, if you're going to watch movies, watch movies that experiment with the filmmaking medium, movies that ask fundamental questions about life and the way we live it, rather than teen comedies or *Star Wars* or whatever. Which led to a long discussion, actually, about whether *Star Wars* was deep or not, and finally Mrs. Glass was forced to admit she had never seen it, and we (the kids) won the argument after making her sit through a long and heated analysis of the relationship between Luke and Leia, the deeper causes of Vader's malevolence, the sexual symbology of Jabba the Hut and all that.

Hee, hee. It was the best discussion we had all week.

None of the other people had seen *any* of them, except for Noel, who'd seen *Dr. Strangelove,* and Grady (one of the senior boys), who'd seen *Citizen Kane.*

Mr. Wallace got all cranked when I told him I knew the movies already, and started (half jokingly) referring to me as a cinema expert. He'd turn to me, in the discussion, and say something like, "Ruby, have you seen *Twelve Monkeys*? Do you want to make any connections for us between that and what Gilliam is doing in *Brazil*?"

And the thing was, I *had* seen *Twelve Monkeys*—twice, actually—and I'd seen most of the other movies he asked me about as well, like *A Clockwork Orange* and *The Shining,* and *The Portrait of a Lady,* so I ended up talking quite a bit in those evening discussions.

Maybe people thought I was annoying or show-offy, talking so much in class.

But I found I didn't care.

Such was the general way things went over the course of the week, but on Wednesday night, when we were discussing *Do the Right Thing,* Noel looked kind of gray in the face. He was sitting next to me, but he was staring down at his shoes, not saying anything.

While Grady and Courtney were disagreeing with each other over the movie, I wrote Noel a note on a scrap of paper. "Do you want to get up early and go see the llamas?" (He hadn't seen them yet.)

He took the note absently, read it and folded it into a tiny square. But he didn't answer.

Halfway through the discussion, he stood up and left

the room. Just waved to Mr. Wallace (who was talking)—not even asking to be excused.

Mrs. Glass followed him.

I sat there as Wallace went on about Gilliam's dystopia in *Brazil* versus Spike Lee's in *Do the Right Thing*, feeling slightly huffy that Noel had ignored my note. Why, after we'd been to *Singin' in the Rain* and pizza and all of that,

after he'd said to me, "You are my thing,"

and signed up for Canoe Island,

and told me about his asthma when he didn't tell anyone else;

after we'd been lab partners and formed the Rescue Squad and eaten lunch together lots of times,

why were we not on more regular friend-type terms? We didn't go to each other's houses, didn't call each other up, didn't hang out on weekends except for that one time.

I mean, why couldn't I pass him a note like a normal friend and get a note back?

●

Thursday morning, when I went to breakfast, Noel was standing in the dining room. At first, I thought, Oh, we're going to the llamas after all—but then I saw that he had his suitcase packed and his sleeping bag in a roll at his feet. He was looking out the window at the water, scanning for the charter ferry on the horizon.

"You're leaving?" I asked.

He nodded.

"Why?"

He cracked a false-looking smile. "The Hooter Rescue Squad needs my expertise."

"What?"

"I got a telegram. There are Seattle hooters in serious danger. I need to bring on my supply of Fruit Roll-Ups."

"Noel, really. How come?"

"What, you don't take the Squad seriously anymore?"

"Noel!"

"I know you're Mission Director, but this assignment came from headquarters in Los Angeles. Hooter-exploitation central."

"Are you really not telling me why you're going?"

He turned away from me. "I just am, okay?"

I backed off. "Okay."

"Not everything is your business, Ruby."

"I said okay." I walked from the dining room into the kitchen, where Mrs. Glass was frying eggs, Mr. Wallace was drinking coffee and Imari was putting strips of bacon onto the grill. I opened a cupboard and pulled out the peanut butter, deliberately starting a conversation about swim team and the meet coming up week after next.

Noel stuck his head in to tell the teachers that the boat was coming into the dock.

"Take care, DuBoise," said Glass.

"I will."

"See you back in school."

And Noel was gone.

At the start of our philosophy discussion, Mr. Wallace announced that someone in Noel's family was sick, and he'd had to go home. Afterward, I so wanted to call him and apologize, but no one besides teachers had been allowed to bring cell phones to Canoe Island, so there wasn't a lot I could do.

●

That evening, before dinner. Me and Nora in the women's sauna.

Varsha and Spencer had just left. We'd been warming up after swim practice. Nora was sweating out her toxins.

Nora: Poor Noel. Did he tell you what happened?
Me: No. Did he tell you?
Nora: No. I only know what Wallace told us.
Me: I hope it's not anything serious.

Nora adjusted her boobs in her swimsuit, the one I saw her buying in the U District that spring. She really does have a great body, when she shows it off.

Her: Do you think . . .
Me: What?
Her: Do you think he'd ever, you know, think of me?
(What?
Oh.
OH.)
Me: You mean, think of you, like a thing?
Her: Uh-huh.
Me: You like him?
Her: Yeah. Yeah, I think I do.
Me: Wow.
Her: No, I definitely do.
Me: Since when?

Her: Kyle's party.

Me: He's shorter than you.

Her: And I'm sure I weigh more than him too. But he's
cute, don't you think?

Me: Sure.

Her: I'm not a size-ist.

I laughed. At five foot eleven, Nora can't afford to
be a size-ist, or there would be hardly any guys for her
to date.

But it hadn't mattered until now, because she hadn't
wanted to go out with anyone.

Her: You guys are such good friends. He hasn't said
anything about me, has he?

Me: No.

Her: Are you sure?

Me: We're really not that good of friends. I don't think
he'd tell me if he had a thing for you.

Her: He wouldn't?

Me: No.

It hadn't occurred to me to think of Noel and Nora.
But now it did. She was kind, and funny, and good at
sports. She had beautiful dark curls and huge hooters. Plus
she could bake.

Every guy's dream. Who on earth would want a neurotic eyeglass leper-slut when he could have a sporty,
mentally stable big-hooter cook?

"He'd be lucky to get you," I said. And I meant it.

"You really think so?"

"Anyone would be lucky to get you," I said. "You're a catch."

Nora smiled and patted my knee. "I should ask him out, then. Because I really like him. Don't you think?"

I felt jealous then. And a little dizzy.

Why?

I liked Angelo.

Didn't I?

Didn't I?

I thought, Rules for Dating in a Small School: If your friend has already said she likes a boy, don't you go liking him too. She's got dibs.

I didn't know how I felt.

Or I did, and I couldn't deal with it.

"I'm getting too hot," I told Nora. "I've gotta go take a shower."

12.

Why Girls Are Better than Boys

1. We are prettier. There's no denying it.
2. We smell better, too.
3. We are loyaler. Is that a word? Maybe not. In any case, we've been your friends since forever, and we *will* be your friends forever, and that what's-his-name is just a momentary obsession we'll all laugh about when we're gray-haired ladies knitting on porch swings. (Although Roo states here and now that she refuses to ever, ever knit, not even when she's eighty.)
4. We will tell you honestly if those jeans make your butt look either weirdly flat or ginormous.
5. We have tampons in our backpacks if you need one.
6. In fact, we also have tissues, gum, lip gloss, nail clippers, combs, extra hair clips, Tylenol and things of that nature, none of which guys *ever* have. Nora even has Band-Aids.

7. We are more likely to stay alive if we fall off an ocean liner. It's true! Women are generally shorter and weaker in the upper body, but we have better endurance, we live longer and we float better. So there.
8. We call when we say we will.

—written by Kim and Roo, together, in Kim's writing. Approximate date: summer after freshman year.

the next day (Friday) after lunch, I skipped Glass's meditation and went for a walk by myself, heading up the hill toward the llamas.

Did I suddenly have feelings for Noel just because my psychology was messed up and I liked a boy I wasn't supposed to like? Or was I even more perverse than that, and liked him now because he was mad at me?

Or had I liked him all along, and liking Angelo was a mere momentary aberration from my true feelings?

I tried thinking of Angelo, and the heart-fluttery, I-like-him-so-much emotion that I'd had before wasn't there. I mean, I still thought he was hot. But it wasn't the same.

I tried thinking of Noel, but the whole thing was so confusing. I couldn't make sense of myself.

When I got to the top of the hill, the llamas were in their pen, eating out of a trough. I couldn't see anybody in the owners' house, so I walked up and took some pellets in my hand. The llamas nuzzled their soft noses at me to get the food, and I stroked their hairy necks.

I stood there for a few minutes, thankful not to be thinking of anything but making the animals feel good and watching the way they pushed each other out of the way in hopes of getting some attention.

Then I heard footsteps on the path behind me, and turned.

It was Kim.

"Ruby," she said. "I was hoping I could talk to you."

Here is how it had been with Kim, in more detail: we seemed to have an agreement to be civil but to keep out of one another's way whenever possible. Like when she came into the sauna and I was there, I got up after a couple of minutes and went to take a shower. Or when I saw she'd decided to do the meditation with Glass, I skipped it.

I had noticed that she avoided Courtney (Jackson's ex) the same way I did, and that she avoided Nora, too. She was mainly with Mei and Sierra, or with some of the sophomores who had rowed crew team with her in the spring. She never sat near me at meals, and when we'd had to cook together, she'd busied herself with a turkey while I made salad, and we'd barely had to speak.

Standing on the path, Kim looked small and alone. One of her knees was muddy, like she'd fallen on her way up the hill, and her hands were dirty too.

"Did you follow me out here?" I asked.

"Kind of, yeah."

"You can feed the llamas if you want," I said. "They'll eat out of your hands."

Kim right away scooped up some feed pellets and stretched her muddy palm out to the biggest llama, the white one.

That's something I had always liked about her. She wasn't timid. The llama sniffed her hand twice and started to eat.

"I owe you an apology," she said finally.

"Oh?"

"I should never have made that Xerox last year. You know, the one with your list of boys on it."

"I know what Xerox you're talking about," I answered. "There was only one Xerox."

"I knew it was private," Kim went on. "And I knew it wasn't what people thought it was. I can't really say what got into me. I was so angry I couldn't see, like everything had gone black."

"Uh-huh."

"And then I wrote stuff on the bathroom wall, and made Cricket and Nora take sides with me, and it was like a way of making the blackness disappear. I don't know if you can understand that."

"I don't think I can," I said. "You ruined my life."

"I know." Kim stopped looking at me and reached down for another handful of feed. "I spent a lot of time thinking about it over the summer, but it wasn't until I was in Tokyo, with no one to talk to, that I really saw how far overboard I went. I should have just yelled at you or something. I mean, we used to be friends."

"Yeah," I said. "We used to."

"Anyhow," she said, looking at me again. "What I did was completely wrong. And I wish I hadn't done it. I shouldn't have put Nora and Cricket in the middle, either."

"Cricket still isn't speaking to me."

"I know." Kim twisted her hands around each other. "I'm really sorry."

"All right," I said. "That's nice to hear, I guess."

"Are you going to forgive me?"

"I don't know," I said. "I don't know if I can forgive you. But I accept the apology. And–" I hesitated, because I didn't really want to apologize for what happened at Spring Fling, when Jackson and I kissed, because Jackson was part of that too–a big part–and he'd been forgiven such a long time ago, as if it wasn't even his fault. It didn't seem fair for me to say I was sorry when he was off the hook, as if he'd had no real agency in the whole thing. "I'm sorry for flirting with Finn," I said finally. "When you two were together. You were right about that."

"Oh," she said. "Thanks."

I knew Kim wasn't going to apologize for taking Jackson away. Because she felt like he was her true love, and to Kim's mind, true love trumped everything.

"I need to tell you," I blurted, not planning to. "I saw Jackson at the zoo with somebody else."

Kim's face fell. "What do you mean?"

"He was out with somebody else. I saw them. They had their arms around each other."

"Why are you telling me?"

I hadn't expected her to ask me that. "I thought you should know," I said, after a second. "That he's stepping out."

Kim's eyes narrowed. "You can't stand it that we're together, can you?"

"What?"

"You don't want me and Jackson to be in love the way we are, do you? So you have to try and ruin everything."

"That's not it."

"I thought we were putting it behind us."

"We are," I said. "That's why I'm telling you."

"I don't know, Ruby. It sounds to me like you want to split us up."

"I saw them together, Kim."

"Look. That girl could have been anyone. You don't know what you saw."

"I'm pretty certain."

"You are? Because you're messing around where it isn't your business, and actually, I don't even believe what you're saying."

"No, I–"

"There are all kinds of reasons you'd make something like that up."

"I'm not making it up."

"I think you are. God, who knew you could be so spiteful after such a long time?"

"Kim, I–"

"Forget it," she said. "Let's just not speak anymore."

"Fine," I said.

"Go, then. Before I say something even worse."

"I'm not going," I found myself saying. "I was here first. You go."

"All right, I will." Kim turned her back on me and ran into the woods. As soon as she was out of sight, I could hear her burst into tears.

I stood there, looking at the llamas, and my heart

started hammering and my neck felt sweaty and suddenly there wasn't enough air in the entire universe to help me breathe. I gasped, and held on to the edge of the pen, and tried to take deep breaths like Doctor Z had taught me.

I told myself, You are not dying. You are just neurotic.

There is plenty of air.

Calm down. It was only an argument. The world isn't coming to an end.

Calm down.

Calm down.

Breathe.

In the end, I made myself focus on the llamas. The way one of them was lying on the ground, with its legs tucked under itself. The way their legs were furry and fat-looking. The way they walked, slightly awkwardly. How their ears pricked up at any sound in the woods.

●

"Mr. Wallace, I need to use your cell phone." I had found him in the kitchen, eating Oreos straight out of the bag with a guilty look on his face. He offered me one, and I took it.

"Is this an emergency?" he asked. "Because this is a *retreat,* you know, from the outside world."

"I need to use it, and then I need to get a call back on it, later on," I said. "Please."

"How come?" He shoved a cookie in his mouth, whole.

"I just have someone I need to talk to."

"Can't it wait?" he asked. "We're going home on Sunday morning."

"No," I answered. "It can't wait."

"Is there something I should know? I'm here to help."

I took a deep breath. "I get panic attacks," I said. "I haven't had any in a while, but I just had one, a bad one, and I need to talk to my shrink."

He took his cell out of his pocket and handed it over. "Give it back when you're done," he said. "I have unlimited minutes."

"This is Doctor Lorraine Zaczkowski. You have reached my answering machine. At the tone, please leave a message with your name and telephone number. You have as long as you need. I'll get back to you as soon as possible. Thank you."

Beep.

"Doctor Z, this is Ruby Oliver. I just really, really need to talk to someone who knows what's going on. I'm on a school retreat, but here's the number."

Then I took the phone and went down to the dock where the boats come in. I curled up in a ball under my jacket, waiting for her to ring.

She called back at seven o'clock. It was dinnertime, and I could see the lights glowing from the lodge a hundred yards away.

"Hello, is this Ruby?"

"Yes."

"Doctor Zaczkowski."

It was so good to hear her voice that I started to cry into the telephone. But as I calmed down and laid it all out—about Kim and the llamas and the apology and the argument—I could feel my body unwind. I uncurled from my ball and stretched out on the dock.

"Do you know why you told Kim about Jackson stepping out?" Doctor Z asked. "It sounds like you're saying that was the moment that changed the course of your interaction."

"Yeah. We were almost getting along before that."

Doctor Z was silent. I could hear her flick a lighter open, then inhale.

"I didn't think she'd get mad," I said. "I thought she'd be grateful for the information."

"You were doing something kind?"

"She didn't see it that way, but yes. I think I was."

"Oh?"

"She thought I was trying to sabotage her and Jackson. Which I can see, I guess. Since I've done it before."

"Back in September you had some complicated feelings about telling Kim that Jackson wrote you notes. Am I right in remembering?"

I thought back. "I wanted to tell because I wanted her to think Jackson still liked me."

"Yes."

"So like it wasn't out of goodness or kindness at all. It was sour and mean."

"Oh?"

"Because I'm neurotic bitter breakup lady and I was trying to make a power move."

"But you didn't end up telling her, did you?" asked Doctor Z.

"No."

"So why did you tell her something similar now? Was it a power move this time?"

"No," I answered honestly. "But I guess coming to Canoe Island at all was. I mean, not a manipulative, evil power move so much as me refusing to lose my friends and not go on the retreat when I wanted to go, just because she was going to be there, too."

"You were standing up for yourself."

"Yeah. But that's not what I was doing when I told about Jackson."

"No?"

"I wasn't showing Kim that Jackson still liked me. I was showing that he *didn't*. That he was with that zoo girl. That in fact, anything between him and me is well and truly over."

I hadn't said that out loud yet.

It sounded good.

"What Jackson was doing with that zoo girl was wrong," I went on. "Plain and simple. And no matter what's between Kim and me, it's bad to have your boyfriend cheating on you."

"You told her out of kindness."

"Because we pledged to tell each other the truth. To tell each other 'all relevant data.' In *The Boy Book*," I answered. "And even if we don't have a friendship anymore, and even if it's not my business, I don't think Kim deserves to be powerless and ignorant when her boyfriend's stepping out."

Doctor Z inhaled cigarette smoke, audibly, and then said the kind of thing she always says. "Is there any way you could tell her that?"

"Duh," I answered. "I could just tell her."

"Um-hm."

"But she might try to kill me. You know that, don't you? I'll be axe-murdered by a venomous exchange-program escapee, and it will be all because of your bad advice."

"Roo," announced Doctor Z, "our hour is up. Do you want to make an appointment for next week?"

"Yes," I answered after a pause. "I do."

●

I went through the last day of Canoe Island in a daze. I couldn't speak to Kim because (1) she was never alone, and (2) I was terrified. But I didn't have any more panic things, and not much happened in general.

When the boat docked in Seattle on Sunday in the late afternoon, and my mom and dad were there jumping up and down in front of the Honda like absolute lunatics, I felt a flood of relief that Canoe Island was over. But I also felt like I had done something, and been somewhere, and proven myself in ways that I hadn't before.

We gave Hutch a ride home because no one had come to pick him up. He said his parents were away on vacation. "Then come to our place for dinner!" cried my dad. "Wait, no, let's go out to Chinese. Judy Fu's Snappy Dragon? Whaddya say?"

Hutch looked at me sideways. "I don't want to barge in on your family outing," he said. "That's cool."

"You should come," I said, making my voice sound warm even though I was actually a little unsure because he's a leper and he sometimes weirds me out—and because for so long, just in principle, I have been essentially anti–John Hutchinson. "They make these excellent fried wontons," I added.

"Oh," Hutch mumbled, in that foggy way of his. "If there are wontons involved, count me in. You didn't say wontons before."

"Wontons, wontons, wontons!" yelled my dad.

And I yelled it after him. "Wontons, wontons, wontons!"

So Hutch came to dinner with us.

And it was okay.

●

If this were a movie of my life, I would go on for a couple of weeks in a state of dejection, after which Noel would appear on my doorstep one day begging forgiveness for being so cranky and hopefully bringing some quality gift. We would kiss somewhere cinematic, like outside in a snowstorm (*Bridget Jones*) or on an ice rink (*Serendipity*) or on a fire escape (*Pretty Woman*). And that would be the end.

But as I have learned, to my disappointment, life is never like the movies. And as I have also learned, thanks to what is now nine months of therapy (with one month-long hiatus): if you don't want to be in an argument with someone, it is probably best to try to solve the problem, rather than lying around hoping the other person will do it for you. Like Doctor Z says, "We can't know or say what other people will do. *You* have to think what *you* want to do to get the situation where you want it to be."

●

Noel wasn't in school Monday. After swim practice, I got Varsha to drop me in the U District, where I bought a CD of goofy frat-rock songs. Then I caught the bus to Noel's house, which took an hour. And I rang his bell.

"Ruby!" cried Mrs. DuBoise, wiping her hands on her apron. She was completely covered in tomato sauce and had a blotch of flour on her cheek. "I am attempting to make pizza. Have you ever made pizza? I have this stone that's supposed to make our regular oven like a pizza oven."

"Cool."

"Noel!" she yelled. "Your friend Ruby is here!"

There was no response. "He's probably gelling his hair," she said, winking. "Noel!" she yelled again.

"What?"

"Ruby is here! Can she come up?"

"I guess so," he yelled down.

"I take no responsibility for his manners." Mrs. DuBoise smiled. "It's like trying to train a tyrannosaur."

"That's okay."

"Are you staying for dinner?" she asked. "I can't vouch for the quality of my pizza, because it's an experiment. But I'm making chicken, too, because Pierre and Mignon will not eat anything that involves tomatoes, even if you bribe them with chocolate."

"Thanks," I said. "But I have to talk to Noel first. We had an argument."

Mrs. DuBoise widened her eyes. "Oooooh. That explains a lot," she said. "All right, then. Up the stairs, second door on the left."

I started up the stairs, then stopped. "Um, Mrs. DuBoise."

"Call me Michelle."

"Is the person okay? The person who was sick in your family, I mean. Who Noel came home for."

She looked confused, and then answered, "Yes, yes. He's fine. Thanks for asking, Ruby."

●

Noel's room was messy. Clothes and books and CD cases were all over the floor. Noel was sitting at his desk, feet up. It looked like he'd been reading a music magazine.

"Hey," I said.

"Hey."

"I came to say I'm sorry," I told him. "For prying into your business."

"I was an asshole," he said.

"No, you weren't. I was being nosy. I do that sometimes. Get into people's business when they don't want."

"Maybe."

"I completely do. But I have good intentions."

"Roo." Noel took his feet off the desk. "I want to tell you something."

"What?"

"The person who was sick in my family—that's what they told you, right? That someone in my family was sick?"

"Yeah."

"Well, it was me."

"What?"

"I've been blowing off my asthma meds and smoking and generally not dealing with this fucking annoying situation with my lungs, because it just . . ." He shrugged. "Anyway. For a couple of years now I've been ignoring it. Wishing it would disappear. And there must have been a ton of pollen or dust or something up on Canoe Island, or maybe I was stressed about something, I don't know, and given that I didn't even bring my anti-inflammatories and smoked like a hundred cigarettes out on the dock, I was having what they call bronchoconstriction. Asthma attacks."

"Oh."

"I couldn't breathe half the time and I kept having to use the puffer way more than I'm supposed to. I was hiding out in the bathroom to do it. It was completely depressing and lame. Finally, I told Wallace and Glass what was going on, but I asked them not to say anything. Not even to you."

"How come?"

"I—I've been so fucking pissed about having this disease. I didn't want to be dealing. It was just embarrassing and stupid, and—" He looked down at his hands. "I didn't handle it well."

"Oh," I answered. "I wouldn't have told anybody."

"I know." Noel sighed. "The point is, I'm *supposed* to tell people. And I'm supposed to take care of it. It's safer if people know. And still I don't tell. I'm like a madman."

I nodded.

"Glass finally called my parents and they made me come home and see the doctor."

"Are you okay?"

"Yeah. I'm not smoking anymore. They gave me a nicotine patch. And I got a new kind of puffer, so that should help. And I'm taking the stupid pills."

"That's good."

"They made me promise I'd start telling people, too. So they can help me out if there's a problem."

"Are you still gonna do cross-country?"

"Yeah. I just have to be not such an angry youth about it. Not taking my meds, et cetera."

I held out the CD, which was in a plastic bag. "I brought you this."

Noel pulled it out and smiled. "Roo! This is excellent." He looked at me, still standing near the door of his room. "Sit down, okay? I promise not to be an angry youth or do any more asthma bitching."

I sat on the floor.

Because the bed just seemed too bedlike.

Noel got down and sat next to me. He pulled the wrapper off the CD and put the disc in his player. "My Sharona" banged through the speakers.

"Ruby?" asked Noel, putting his hand on my knee.

"Yeah?"

"Um."

"What?"

"Can I kiss you?"

I wanted him to.

I so wanted him to.

It was like Angelo and Jackson and every other boy I'd ever kissed had flown out of my mind, leaving only Noel.

But I shook my head. "No."

"Oh," he said, pulling his hand off my knee and looking down. "Sorry. I kind of thought things were going that way."

"I thought they were, too," I said. "They were."

"But they're not?"

"No."

"Is it 'cause you have a boyfriend?"

"What? What boyfriend?"

"I heard it from Jackson."

"When did you hang out with Jackson?"

"We're on cross-country together." Noel shrugged. "I heard him tell Kyle in the locker room."

"And he said–"

"That you had a boyfriend. Some Garfield guy named Angelo."

I didn't want to confess my lie. It was too psycho. "Oh, *Angelo*. That was just a little nothing thing," I explained. "It's over now."

"Oh." Noel brushed my lips with his index finger. "So maybe I *can* kiss you?" He leaned forward. "Because I've been wanting to for a really long time."

I pulled back. "I can't."

He stroked my hair. "Why not? If things are going that way, like you said."

"I get panic attacks," I said, shifting myself away. "Do you know what those are?"

"Kind of, yeah."

"I have to see a shrink because I freak out about stuff," I said. "And I've been trying to figure out why I do things, and why I feel like I feel, and how I ended up not having any friends for such a long time."

He looked at me as if asking me to go on.

"And I just last month made up with Nora, and she finally wants to be friends with me after everything that happened, and, well–we have a code."

"Like what?"

"Like we can't take up with a guy if someone else likes him first."

Noel paused. And then said: "I see."

"She's my friend, and I don't want to lose her like I

lost Kim and Cricket, and I'm trying to figure out how to be a good person, and it doesn't always come naturally to me."

"I think you're a good person," said Noel.

"Sometimes I am," I answered. "And this is one of those times."

"Oh."

"So I'm really sorry, but I don't think there's anything else to do." I stood up. "I should probably go."

"Yeah," he said. "You probably should."

It was one of the hardest things I've ever done, but I turned and walked out the door.

●

Tuesday, I went to school with *The Boy Book* wrapped in some old Santa Claus paper. On it was a note I had written:

Dear Kim,

We were friends once.

I doubt we'll be friends again. Too much has happened. But maybe we can remember what it used to be like without such a ginormous quantity of bitterness.

So I want you to have this book.

I was telling you the truth the other day. I know sometimes I am sour mean bitter breakup lady, but sometimes I am also loyal truth-telling lady who messes in business that's not her own. But only because she really can't stand it when bad stuff is going on.

Anyway.

Here's The Boy Book.

Brava for Kaptain Kangaroo. May she rest in peace.

—Roo

183

I left it in her mail cubby, though I had to squash it in order to get it in. It was easier than giving it to her in person.

And I felt relieved.

Like that whole era of my life was over.

Like *The Boy Book* and everything it stood for—me, Nora and Cricket and Kim—was done with. And the thoughts inside it too.

Some of them were worth remembering. The front-close bra and not sunbathing topless and the clever comebacks to catcalls. But most of it was in the past.

It was a document of how I used to think. When I was, sort of, someone else.

13.

The Girl Book: A Disorganized Notebook of Thoughts, with No Particular Purpose, Written Purely for the Benefit of Me, Ruby Oliver, and My Mental Health

Nancy Drews.
    That is, things I am good at.[1]

1. The backstroke. Not great, but decent and getting better.
2. Talking. I'm like my mom that way.
3. Making lists. I really could medal in this one.
4. Movies. Remembering trivia and being able to say semi-intelligent stuff about cinema when called upon to do so.
5. Getting animals to like me. And not being afraid of them.

---

[1] A homework assignment from Doctor Z, which she shrinkily calls a list of affirmations, but which I prefer to term Nancy Drews, because Nancy Drew, girl detective, was good at everything, even horseback riding and water ballet, though there was no evidence she had ever practiced or even heard of either one until she miraculously turned out to be expert at them.

6. Reading mystery novels. Which is not that hard. But I do it fast.

7. Writing stuff down in such a way that it is at least moderately amusing.

8. School, generally. With the exception of math, which, if I am honest, I just don't care about at all.

9. Painting pictures of animals that semi-resemble the actual animal that I am trying to paint. Human bodies still elude me, as proven by multiple attempts in Advanced Painting Elective—and my landscapes suck, as do my pictures of fruit. But when I paint something by myself, from a photo in one of my animal books or just from memory, it comes out pretty good. Not that I do it that often.

10. I am good at giving presents.

11. And finding clothes in vintage shops.

12. And being a good friend. At least, I am getting better.

—written by me, Ruby Oliver, all by myself. Exact date: November 21, junior year.

Meghan broke up with Bick at Thanksgiving. He cried and begged her not to.

It was very satisfying to hear about, but Meghan was sad. Because she loves him. But she told him that the long-distance thing, whether they were faithful or taking it one day at a time, was making her insane. And she hated thinking that she had to go to college in Boston, when she might want to go somewhere and study singing, or skip college and train to be a yoga teacher, or go to school somewhere warm by the beach. And she didn't actually think they'd ever get married, and she didn't want to think about getting married now anyway, and there wasn't any point to it anymore.

She couldn't live her life in Seattle with her heart and mind at Harvard, she told him.

Nora and I took her out for espresso milk shakes to make her feel better. Then we went and saw a big cheesy movie with alien invaders, and slept over at the Van Deusens'.[2]

Kim said thank you for *The Boy Book,* and we had a little fake hug, and then went back to pretty much ignoring each other, only now we said hi in the halls and I could go to parties without angsting that something awful would happen. She and Cricket became fully enmeshed in the Katarina-Heidi-Ariel set, and Nora stayed on the fringes, mainly hanging out with me and Meghan.

●

Kim and Jackson stayed together. What I heard from Nora (who made up with Kim quickly after Canoe Island) was that Kim confronted him, and there was really quite a scene, but he broke things off with the zoo girl and told Kim he was incredibly sorry and had just been so confused and lonely that he'd made a big mistake. And he wrote her notes and gave her a Hello Kitty lunch box and a cashmere sweater. So she forgave him.

I never told her about the notes he wrote me, or how he invited me to Kyle's party.

I decided it wasn't my business to tell.

---

2 Nora's brother, Gideon, the one who goes to Evergreen, was there—home for Thanksgiving break. I think Gideon is extremely hot, even though Nora claims his eyebrows grow together in a truly disgusting fashion. Anyway, I caught him staring at my legs when we got in the hot tub. So that put me in a good mood.

And besides, Jackson was fully cured of his tendency to flirt with me or try to get me to forgive him, or whatever it was, by the obvious fact that it was I who spilled the beans to his girlfriend about his stepping out with the zoo girl.

Things were awkward between me and Noel for a few weeks, but after that it got a little better. We stayed Chem lab partners, but he stopped sending me e-mails. We ate lunch together on the Chemistry days, but we always found other people to sit with, too. Sometimes he came out to the movies with me and Meghan and Nora, but we never went anywhere alone, and we never talked on the phone. The Hooter Rescue Squad was officially defunct.

I never told Nora what happened when I went to his house with the CD.

Noel didn't like Nora, not that way. She would sometimes sit next to him on purpose, or look at him for a long time like she wasn't keeping track of the lunch conversation, and I could tell she still liked him.

Besides which, she told me she did. She said he was interesting, and funny, and she liked the way his hair stood up.

And I had to agree.

She said he was outside the Tate Universe, at least more than everyone else was, and that the guys at Tate were generally too pigheaded and sexist. And even those who weren't were manly-manly preppy future doctors of America.

Muffins.

Which was true.

But Nora never got the courage to ask Noel out. When I hinted around about it, she kept saying she would. But then she didn't. A senior from the basketball team tried to scam on her at a party Heidi Sussman had in early December. Nora kissed the guy for a short time in the kitchen, but then she complained she was tired and went home, never to really deal with him again.

●

I retrained for penguin-lecture-giving at the zoo and redeemed myself in Anya's eyes on the next go-round. I started to like the Family Farm part of the job as well. Me and Laverne and Shirley got pretty close. And after a while, I asked to do less gardening and more stuff with the animals, so Anya let me help muck out the farm animal pens instead of gardening. Which was gross, but anyway.

Of course, all my money went to paying back my parents for Canoe Island, so I was broke until the new year.

●

My parents were happy that I was dealing with my issues in therapy with Doctor Z, and continued to speculate on whether I was a lesbian.

And to remind me that they were okay with that.

"I'm not a lesbian, you guys," I'd say.

"It's a perfectly normal way to be, sweetie."

"Yeah, only I'm not."

"It's normal to be in denial, too. Just be true to yourself," one of them would say, and then we'd have a long dinner conversation for my benefit about all the gay friends my mother has, and her possibly lesbian relationship with Lisa from high school, and movies they'd seen and liked with gay characters in them, and famous people who were gay. Then my dad would give me some meaningless compliment—how pretty I am or what an interesting person I am—in hopes of boosting my self-esteem. And I would look at my plate and stir my pasta around, waiting for the meal to be over.

Ag.

A few days after Canoe Island, Hutch asked Noel if he wanted to go see Aerosmith in concert, and Noel said yes, and they went and did manly bonding things involving rock music. So the two of them started hanging out a bit. And though Hutch's leper status didn't improve much beyond that, and his skin didn't either, he sat with us at lunch now and then. And it was okay, so long as he didn't quote obscure retro metal lyrics that no one understood.

We went back to being partners in French.

Angelo fell in love with his new girlfriend. Her name was Jade. Juana told my mother, and my mother (completely ignorant of my adventures with Angelo) told me. She said Angelo brought Jade home for dinner and she was really charming and smart, and Angelo just looked at her like the sun was shining through her eyes.

And I didn't feel a thing when I heard about it. Except glad for him.

We had to have dinner together sometimes, just like we always had. But we sat on opposite sides of the couch when we were watching TV, and I always wore a back-close bra and a dress, just to stay on the safe side. Because when I looked at the excellence of Angelo's profile, I did start to remember his proficiency in the boob-groping department and got a little tempted. But then I'd just pet a rottweiler or a shih tzu or something and make some comment about reality TV, and the moment would be over.

●

And me. Ruby Oliver. I started *The Girl Book*. Excerpt at the start of this chapter. It's like a free-for-all notebook for stuff that I'm thinking. I made a cover for it with a painting of Humboldt penguins, gouache on construction paper, and it doesn't look half bad. My dad bought a new computer and gave me his old one, so I used that to write down all the things that happened at the start of this school year, which is what you're reading now.

I swim. And I go see Doctor Z. And I work my zoo job. And I write stuff. I rent movies with my girlfriends and drink espresso milk shakes at the B&O.

I don't think about Jackson at all anymore. I see him in the halls, and my radar is gone. He's a pod-robot and I don't care.

I do not care.

I do not care.

I see Kim, and there is still an ache for the kind of friends we used to be. Because I don't have that with anyone, the way I did with her. And maybe I never will.

Maybe friendships aren't like that when we get older.

But the Kim ache is dull. Not a surge of immediate panicky pain and anger like it used to be. It's an ache for what happened in the past, not what's happening now.

I can live with it.

And I do.

If I am sad about anything, and sometimes I am, it is Noel. I talk about him a lot in therapy. Because I think there could have been something, a real thing, between us. And now there is just a low-level friendship that will never get any deeper. At least, I don't think it will.

I made the right decision. But that doesn't mean I don't have any regrets.

●

The first night of winter break, I had Meghan and Nora sleep over at my house.

I almost never have anyone sleep over. I hardly ever did, even before the debacles of sophomore year. Our place is so much smaller than where my friends live, and the walls are thin. Why would you sleep on the floor in the living room of a semibohemian houseboat when you can have hot tubs and swimming pools and bedroom-bathroom suites?

The answer was always obvious: you wouldn't.

But I invited them anyway, because Meghan was going away to visit her grandparents for the holidays, so we wouldn't see her for two weeks. And they came.

My parents went to Juana's for dinner, and Nora made nachos and chocolate chip cookies, and the three of us played Trivial Pursuit, Silver Screen Edition, which I'd bought for myself after spending a horror-filled evening with the four-year-old vomit machine I used to babysit. (I kicked some serious butt at Trivial Pursuit, by the way, even when Meghan and Nora teamed up against me.)

Then we put mud masks on our faces and Meghan painted her toenails and Nora looked at my dad's flower photograph books and I cleaned up the kitchen so my parents wouldn't have a fit when they got home.

They arrived, and my dad was tipsy and pretended to be terrified at our green-mud faces, and they made a lot of noise going in and out of the bathroom brushing their teeth, and then they left us alone.

We made a big extended bed on the living room floor with couch cushions, three pillows and sleeping bags Nora and Meghan had brought over, plus my bedclothes and a lot of extra sheets. It was like fifteen feet wide. We washed the mud off our faces, put on pajamas and got in to watch *Saturday Night Live*.

The show was kind of boring, and Meghan fell asleep five minutes into it. Nora, on my other side, went out a couple of minutes later.

I lay there in the blue light from the TV set. Not really watching. Just lying there, between Meghan and Nora.

Meghan snored softly.

Nora was breathing through her mouth and drooling onto the pillow.

The TV went to a commercial and I switched it off with the remote.

The water lapped at the sides of our houseboat.

And I felt lucky.

acknowledgments

Thank you to Marissa for hacking out the boring footnotes and making the whole thing so much better. And to Beverly, Chip, Kathleen and everyone else at Delacorte Press, especially the sales force, for all their hard work and support of my books. I am always and muchly in debt to Elizabeth for her stellar and unflagging representation.

I am grateful to the people in my YA novelists newsgroup for their wonderful humor and insight about the publishing and writing process.

Thank you also to the FOZ (friends of Zoe)—Julia, Anne, Vanessa and Mika—who gamely took the John Belushi pop-reference quiz, thus enabling this book to be (hopefully) full of footnotes and film references that are entertaining and semi-informative, rather than un-. Most of all, my appreciation to Zoe, quiz administrator extraordinaire, who also helped me figure out how to end the book.

Thanks to Bellamy Pailthorp and Melissa Greeley for helping me get the Seattle details right, though I know I completely reinvented the Woodland Park Zoo for my own literary purposes.

My love and thanks to my immediate family and felines, although for accuracy's sake it must be noted that the cat Mercy Randolph caused more problems than she solved.

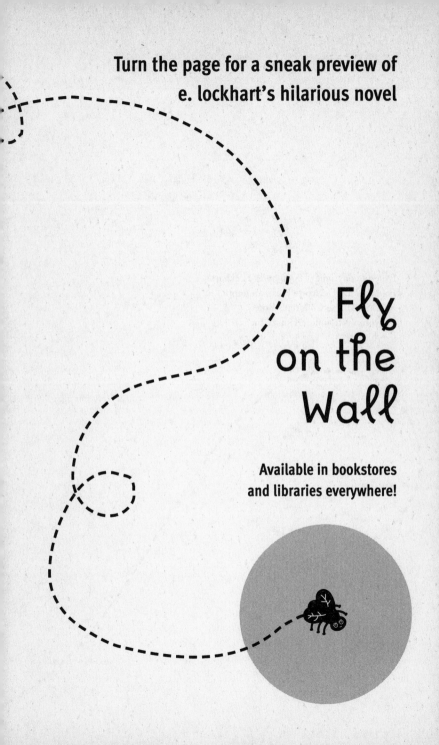

**Turn the page for a sneak preview of
e. lockhart's hilarious novel**

Fly
on the
Wall

**Available in bookstores
and libraries everywhere!**

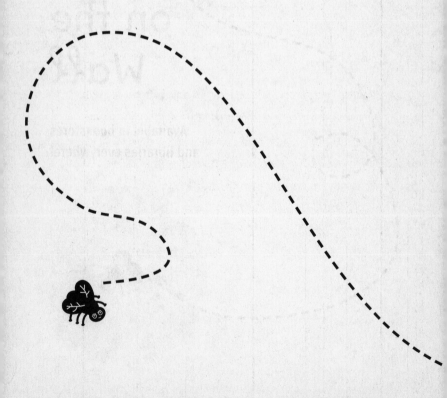

Fly on the Wall: *How One Girl Saw Everything* is about a girl called Gretchen Kaufman Yee who goes to a wacked-out art school in New York City. Gretchen is a collector of plastic Chinese food and odd figurines, a passionate comic-book artist, and a crazy Spider-Man fanatic. She's also completely freaked out by the opposite sex—in particular, the Art Rats, a group of guys in her drawing concentration. One day, she wishes she could be a "fly on the wall of the boys' locker room," just to find out what the heck guys are really talking about.

And the next thing she knows . . . she is.

A fly.

On the wall of the boys' locker room.

"I think this might be the best YA novel, as in a book published for young adults and also written for young adults, that I've ever read. Because it's a reworking of Kafka, and it's this crazy brilliant upending of all the sexual stereotypes we've ever had—particularly in YA lit—and it's hilarious, and it's so very smart. I mean, I'm serious. . . . It's really amazing." —John Green, winner of the Michael L. Printz Award for *Looking for Alaska*

friday. I am eating alone in the lunchroom.

Again.

Ever since Katya started smoking cigarettes, she's hanging out back by the garbage cans, lighting up with the Art Rats. She bags her lunch, so she takes it out there and eats potato chips in a haze of nicotine.

I hate smoking, and the Art Rats make me nervous. So here I am: in my favorite corner of the lunchroom, sitting on the floor with my back against the wall. I'm eating fries off a tray and drawing my own stuff—not anything for class.

Quadriceps. Quadriceps.
Knee.
Calf muscle.
Dull point; must sharpen pencil.
Hell! Pencil dust in fries.
Whatever. They still taste okay.
Calf muscle.
Ankle.
Foot.
KA-POW! Spider-Man smacks Doctor Octopus off the edge of the building with a swift kick to the jaw. Ock's face contorts as he falls backward, his metal tentacles flailing with hysterical fear. He has an eighty-story fall beneath him, and—
Spidey has a great physique. Built, but not too built. Even if I did draw him myself.

I think I made his butt too small.

Do-over.

I wish I had my pink eraser, I don't like this white one.

Butt.

Butt.

Connecting to: leg . . . and . . . quadriceps.

There. A finished Spidey outline. I have to add the suit. And some shadowing. And the details of the building. Then fill in the rest of Doc Ock as he hurtles off the edge.

Mmmm. French fries.

Hell again! Ketchup on Spidey.

Lick it off.

Cammie Holmes is staring at me like I'm some lower form of life.

"What are you looking at?" I mutter.

"Nothing."

"Then. Stop. Staring," I say, sharpening my pencil again, though it doesn't need it.

This Cammie is all biscuits. She's stacked like a character in a comic book. Cantaloupes are strapped to her chest.

Her only redeeming quality.

"Why are you licking your Superman drawing?" Cammie tips her nose up. "That's so kinky. I mean, I've heard of licking a centerfold, but licking Superman?"

"Spider."

"What?"

"*Spider*-Man."

"Whatever. Get a life, Gretchen."

She's gone. From across the lunchroom comes her nasal voice: "Taffy, get this: I just caught Gretchen Yee giving oral to some Superman drawing she made."

Spider. Spider. Spider-Man.

"She *would*." Taffy Johnson. Stupid tinkly laugh.

Superman is a big meathead. I'd never draw Superman. Much less give him oral.

I haven't given anybody oral, anyway.

I hate those girls.

Taffy is doing splits in the middle of the lunchroom floor, which is just gross. Who wants to see her crotch like that? Though of course everybody does, and even if they didn't, she wouldn't care because she's such a unique spirit or whatever.

I hate those girls, and I hate this place: the Manhattan High School for the Arts. Also known as Ma-Ha.

Supposedly, it's a magnet high school for students talented in drawing, painting, sculpture or photography. You have to submit a portfolio to get in, and when I did mine (which was all filled with inks of comic-book characters I taught myself to draw in junior high) and when I finally got my acceptance letter, my parents were really excited. But once you're here, it's nothing but an old, ugly New York public school building, with angry teachers and crap facilities like any other city public school—except I've got drawing class every day, painting once a week and art history twice. I'm in the drawing program.

Socially, Ma-Ha is like the terrible opposite of the schools you see on television, where everyone wants to be the same as everyone else. On TV, if you don't conform and wear what the popular kids are wearing, and talk like they talk, and act like they do—then you're a pariah.

Here, everyone wants to be different.

People have mohawks and dreadlocks and outrageous thrift-store clothes; no one would be caught dead in ordinary jeans and a T-shirt, because they're all so into expressing their individuality. A girl from the sculpture program wears a sari every day, even though her family's Scandinavian. There's that kid who's always got that Pink Panther doll sticking out of her jacket pocket; the boy who smokes using a cigarette holder like they did in forties movies; a girl who's shaved her head and pierced her cheeks; Taffy, who does Martha Graham–technique modern dance and wears her leotard and sweats all day; and Cammie, who squeezes herself into tight goth outfits and paints her lips vampire red.

They all fit in here, or take pride in not fitting in, if

that makes any sense—and if you're an ordinary person you've got to do *something* at least, like dye your hair a strange color, because nothing is scorned so much as normalcy. Everyone's a budding genius of the art scene; everyone's on the verge of a breakthrough. If you're a regular-looking person with regular likes and dislikes and regular clothes,

and you can draw so it looks like the art in a comic book,

but you can't "express your interior life on the page," according to Kensington (my drawing teacher),

and if you can't "draw what you see, rather than imitate what's in that third-rate trash you like to read" (Kensington again),

then you're nothing at Ma-Ha.

Nothing. That's me.

Gretchen Kaufman Yee. Ordinary girl.

Two months ago I capitulated to nonconformity-conformity and had my hair bleached white and then dyed stop-sign red. It cost sixty dollars and it pissed off my mother, but it didn't work.

I'm still ordinary.

I take literature second period with Glazer. I rarely do the reading. I don't like to admit that about myself; I'd like to be the person who does the reading—but I don't.

It seems like I've always got some new comic to read on the subway, and the homework for drawing is more interesting.

In literature, I can't concentrate because Titus Antonakos sits next to me at the big rectangular table. He's an Art Rat, meaning he's one of the boys in the sophomore drawing program, group B. He's delicious and smart and graceful and hot. White skin, with high cheekbones and messy dark hair. Lips like a Greek statue–a little too full for the rest of his face. He's got a retro Johnny Rotten look; today he's wearing a green vinyl jacket, an ironic "I heart New York" T-shirt, jeans and combat boots. He's thin to the point that he's off some other girls' radar, but not mine.

He is absolutely on my radar.

Titus.
Titus.
Titus.
Touch my arm by accident like you did yesterday.
Notice me.
Notice me.

"Gretchen?" It's Glazer.

"Huh?"

"Vermin." She's obviously repeating herself. She sounds annoyed. "The word. I asked you to define it."

"It's a bug, right?" I say. "Like a cockroach."

"It can be," says Glazer, smirking. "Most people do assume that Kafka had his protagonist, Gregor Samsa, turn into a cockroach. That's the standard interpretation of 'The Metamorphosis.' But if you all turn to page five, you'll see that the word Kafka used in German—and the word in our translation—is not *cockroach* or *bug,* but *vermin*—a 'monstrous vermin,' Kafka says—which can be taken to mean any kind of animal, especially those that are noxious or repellent in some way: rats, mice, lice, flies, squirrels."

No idea what she is talking about. I just know the story is about some guy who turns into a bug.
Whatever.
Titus.
Titus.
Titus.
God, he smells good.

"Titus?" Glazer, calling on him. He actually put his hand up.

"Doesn't it also mean disgusting *people*?" Titus says. "Like you could say people who—I don't know—molest kids or steal from their mothers—they're vermin."

"Absolutely." Glazer lights up. "And by extension, you sometimes see the word used as a derogatory term for the masses—for large groups of ordinary people. Or for prisoners. It expresses contempt. Now: why would

Kafka use such a word to describe Gregor's meta-morphosis?"

Titus did the reading.
He just seems good, somehow.
Like the core of him is good when the core of other people is dark, or sour. Like he'd do the reading even if no one was checking, because he cares about stuff.
I wish he didn't hang with those Art Rats. I have class with them every single day, but I can't figure those guys out.
Because they're boys, I guess, and because they try so hard to seem slick and sure. They're nice one minute and cruel the next.
And with Shane around all the time, I can't talk to Titus.
At least, I can't talk and make any sense.
Truth: with Shane around I can't talk to anyone.

The bell. "Finish through page sixty for Monday and enjoy the weekend," calls Glazer. A rustle of books and backpacks.

"Hey, Titus." My voice sounds squeaky. (Shane, thank goodness, is out the door.)

"Yeah?" His mouth looks so soft.

"Oh, I—"

Hell. Was I going to say something? Did I have something to say?
Oh hell,
oh hell,

he's looking right at me, I've got nothing to say.

"Do you–"

What?
What?

"–do you remember what the Kensington is?"

Titus bends over to pick his pencil off the floor. There's a strip of skin between his shirt and the top of his jeans in the back. I can see the top of his boxers. Plain light blue. "Sketch three sculptures of the human body at the Met, remember?"

Of course I remember. If I had a single bone in me I'd ask him to go there on Saturday with me.

I should ask him.
I should ask him.
I should ask him.

"Oh, right," I say. "That's it. Thanks."

Oh! I am a coward!
Spineless, boneless, vermin girl.

"Sure. See you in gym." I try to smile at him but it's too late. He's gone.

Later that afternoon, Sanchez the gym teacher makes us play dodgeball, which leaves bruises all over my legs. I'm not that fast, and I get hit a lot. Titus hits me twice.

"Do you think it means something?" I ask Katya after gym, sitting on the locker room bench in a towel.

Katya is naked in the shower like that's a normal way to have a conversation. She's washing her hair like she's just everyday naked in front of people.

Well, we *are* everyday naked in front of people. Gym is five days a week, shower required. But anyway, Katya is having a naked conversation like it doesn't even bother her, which it obviously doesn't—even though she's not built like a model, just regular.

The locker room is so cramped and tiny that I can feel the warm spray of her shower water on my knee as I'm sitting on the bench.

"It would have meant something if we were sixth graders," says Katya, scrunching her eyes as she rinses out the shampoo.

"Like what would it mean?"

"You want to hear me say it?" She's laughing.

"Yes."

"It would have meant that he liked you back."

"I didn't say I liked him," I mutter.

"Oh please," Katya says, ignoring my point, "that's very sixth grade. You know, how boys were always teasing the girls they liked, pulling their hair. But we're way too old for that crap now. So I don't think it means anything if he hits you with the dodgeball. Sorry."

Katya is always such a realist. She's soaping her underarms like she's alone. I could never do that.

I make a quick dive out of my towel and into my bra and a T-shirt from the second Spider-Man movie, covered with pastel dust. "I didn't say I liked him," I say again.

"Oh, don't give me that."

"What? I'm analyzing the cruel and particularly complicated sociodynamics of sophomore dodgeball."

"No, you're not." Katya is drying off now. In the next row over, annoying Taffy is stretching and showing off her dancer's body while listening to our conversation. I hate this tiny-ass locker room.

"What, it's that obvious?" I ask.

"It's all over your face, all the time," Katya says, grinning. "Titus, Titus, Titus."

I'm blushing. I can feel it. And my Chinese half makes it so that once my cheeks go pink, they stay that way for hours.

Katya never turns pink. Broad, Russian American face and a lumpy nose and long pale brown hair—you wouldn't think she'd be pretty if you made a list of her features, but somehow she is. She's mysterious. You can't read what she's thinking.

"Well, he's better than the others," I say, conscious of Taffy in the next row, trying to sound less obsessed.

"Whatever."

"He is. Let's be objective. He's cuter than Brat Parker. Nicer than Adrian Ip. More interesting than Malachy."

"What's wrong with Malachy?" Katya sounds annoyed.

"He never says anything. Like having his ears pierced makes him so slick he doesn't have to talk."

"You don't have to be so mean about everyone, Gretchen."

"I'm not being mean. I'm doing an objective comparison of the Art Rats."

Which isn't true. I *am* being mean.

I feel mean. I don't know why. This school is making me evil, maybe.

"It's not objective. It's *subjective*." Katya hooks her bra behind her back. "It's just what you think, not the truth."

"Don't bite me, Katya. I'm only talking."

"Well, you're talking about people you barely know."

"I know them. They've been in practically every class with me all year. I know Shane."

"We all know you know Shane. Enough with Shane." Katya gets into a dress she made herself on her mother's sewing machine.

"Wanna get a slice?" I try changing the subject.

"Can't. I've got to pick the monsters up at day care."

I wish she didn't have three little sisters. Wish she didn't live an hour-fifteen away from school on the F train, all the way in Brighton Beach.

"You're always busy these days," I say, and it comes out pitiful and whiny.

"That's life, Gretchen," snaps Katya. "I've got responsibilities. I'll call you later."

She's out the door. My only friend, really.

I can't count Shane, even though we said we'd be friends after last October.

We're not, obviously.

Not friends.

Just people who groped each other for a few weeks at the start of this year, when he was new and sat in front of me in math. One day, he wrote me a note about this nose picker sitting in the front,

and we wrote notes back and forth about boogers,

which led to notes back and forth about other stuff,

and he ate lunch with me and Katya,

and put funny sketches in my locker,

and we were friends. I thought.

But one day Shane walked out of school with me when classes were over,

and got on the subway with me,

and went home with me, without me even asking him.

He kissed me as soon as we got in the door. We made out
on the couch, when my parents weren't home,
    and watched TV on the couch together when they were.
    After that, we made out in the hallways of Ma-Ha,
    by the boat pond in Central Park,
    on the corner by the subway stop,
    and in the back of a movie theater.
    People saw us. And he was my boyfriend. For a little.
    Now, he's just someone whose mouth I stuck my tongue in,
    someone whose spit got all over me and I didn't mind at
the time.
    Now, he's an alien being,
    just like all the rest of those Art Rat boys—
    or even more than the rest.
    It goes to show that if you only have two friends in a
whole godforsaken poseur high school, you shouldn't start up
kissing one of them, because three weeks later he'll say he
doesn't feel that way,
    whatever way that was,
    didn't feel like drooling on me anymore, I guess is what it
meant—
    and he'll say, "Hey, it was fun and all, but let's cool it
now, yeah?"
    and "You know we'll always be friends, right? Excellent.
Let's hang out sometime, Gretchen, that would be great,"
    only not with kissing,
    and not with it meaning anything,

and then, when it comes down to it, never actually hanging out,

and never being friends again, unless people ask and then we both say:

"Yeah, we had a thing going for a few weeks there, but then we both decided we would just be friends."

Only he's *the one who decided.*

And we're not friends, not anymore.

Now he's got the Art Rats and goes out with Jazmin, and little Gretchen Yee isn't worth his time, like she was when he was new in school and lonely.

Hell.

I'll get my stupid slice of pizza by myself, then.